Also by Charles Baxter

Blood Test

Blood Test

A COMEDY

Charles Baxter

Pantheon Books, New York

All rights reserved. Published in the United States by Pantheon Books, a division of Penguin Random House LLC, New York, and distributed in Canada by Penguin Random House Canada Limited, Toronto.

Pantheon Books and colophon are registered trademarks of Penguin Random House LLC.

Library of Congress Cataloging-in-Publication Data
Names: Baxter, Charles, [date]
Title: Blood test / Charles Baxter.
Description: First Edition. | New York: Pantheon Books, 2024.
Identifiers: LCCN 2023048522 (print) |
LCCN 2023048523 (ebook) | ISBN 9780593700853 (hardcover) |
ISBN 9780593700860 (ebook)
Subjects: LCGFT: Novels.
Classification: LCC PS3552.A854 B56 2024 (print) |
LCC PS3552.A854 (ebook) | DDC 813/.54—dc23/eng/20231016
LC record available at https://lccn.loc.gov/2023048522
LC ebook record available at https://lccn.loc.gov/2023048523

www.pantheonbooks.com

Jacket illustration and design by Tyler Comrie

Printed in the United States of America
First Edition
2 4 6 8 9 7 5 3 1

For Dean Bakopoulos,
William Lychack,
and
Pua Johnson

Part I

Who is sitting in that empty chair?

—Eugene Ormandy

1

LET'S SAY YOU STABBED YOURSELF IN THE LEG BY ACCIDENT. LET'S SAY you're bleeding all over the floor.

You'll need a doctor. In this town, to get to the clinic you go down the main street, turn right at the stoplight, and then just one block up ahead, past the strip mall, you'll see it. Its big glass sliding front doors are wide enough for two wheelchairs going in opposite directions to pass each other, and there's a good-sized parking lot out front for the sickos and their relatives. The spaces are usually filled. We have a lot of near-dead people in these parts. You can see them staggering in, breathing hard, young and old, propped up by their canes or walkers, accompanied by oxygen tanks, a real ghoul parade. Even the one-eyed badass tatted guys are hobbling in. It's probably the postindustrial air we breathe here, or maybe the nitrate-scented water we drink out of the tap. Could be herbicides we spray on everything or the fact that a third of the town has a drinking problem, and another third is on meth and/or Oxy. You fall down here in Kingsboro, Ohio, you're in good company. It's a grand party of the infirm down there on the ground.

A healthy person over the age of twenty-five acquires a certain charisma in this locale.

I went to the clinic because I hadn't been feeling too good lately. It was ironic. From nine to five, I sit in my office—I sell insurance, including some health insurance—making calls and drawing up policies, sometimes going out to inspect the damages. It's okay work, not too demanding, and I have two assistants. Apart from the occasional natural disasters (tornadoes, fires, hailstones) and the claims that keep me busy now and then, I get to go home, make dinner for my two teenagers and their associates, watch something on TV or browse the internet, say my prayers, and that's it for the day.

But lately I'd been having this pain in my side like someone was stabbing me, but carefully and gently probing for an organ or two. For variety it took up residence in my back. Finally I gave myself two hours off for an exam. I don't like doctors and their godlike attitudes but sometimes they're unavoidable when you feel the way I did.

So there I was in the Kingsboro Medical Clinic sitting on the examining table. I was in my boxer shorts and my undershirt, which I'd been ordered to strip down to by a grim-faced nurse wearing a cheap rhinestone pin. She'd also taken my blood pressure, and she did not like me. Eventually the doctor came in. I didn't know her. She was middle-aged, hair going gray, silver frame glasses hanging from one of those chains. She gave me a split-second semi-smile. My usual doc was out for the day at the Kingsboro Country Club, probably motoring around in her banana-yellow golf cart. Doctors don't have to explain anything to you because they're doctors and you aren't. This doctor's name tag said she was Dr. Janet Hasselblad, like the camera. She introduced herself, asked me how I was doing. She was looking at my chart or whatever it was before she glanced up at me.

"So, Mr. Hutson," she said.

"*Hobson*," I said. "Brock Hobson." She put on her reading glasses and checked my name on her clipboard.

"Sorry," she said. "The print was a little smeared. You have a strange name, if you don't mind my saying. I've never known a

Hobson before. Or a Brock, either." She tried unsuccessfully to smile. "So you're unique. No, that's not right. I once knew a dog named Brock. A cairn terrier, if I remember correctly."

"Oh, that's okay," I said, being affable under duress. I told her what was wrong with me, and she examined my left side while I explained myself.

She asked me some more questions before delivering her opinion. "It's probably diverticulitis," she said, conveying a certain lack of interest as she pushed in the flesh above my hip on my left side (yes, it hurt, thanks), "but we'll have to test it. And your back— that's also probably sciatica, and coincidental, but we'll have to X-ray you to make sure about both of them. They may be stress related." She had a very brisk manner, as if I was her umpteenth patient of the day and medically uninteresting. My body's problems were all in a day's work for her. If I had had cancer, I might have been more intriguing, more of a mystery to be solved. Her advice: I should get more exercise, eat more raw vegetables, take Metamucil, relax, and subject myself to an antibiotic she was about to prescribe. I should also be careful not to get sick with the latest virus. But I have had all my shots! Why wouldn't she smile at me? She wrote down the order for the tests, also the prescription, told me that she would be back in a minute, and that I should get my clothes back on.

When she returned, she handed me two pieces of paper, lab orders. She had another piece of paper that she did not give to me. Private doctor insider info: Am I well groomed, etc.? I would have liked to see my chart, but they don't care to disclose it. That's private, insider MD stuff. She explained about the blood and urine tests, an X-ray to make sure that I had what she thought I had, another X-ray for my back trouble: all standard practice. Insurance would cover most of it, she said, as if I didn't know what was covered and what wasn't. She repeated herself and told me I should exercise more, take walks, watch my diet, avoid unpleasant situations, abstain from excessive alcoholism. Yes, fine. After I took these tests, she would see me again, she told me, a follow-up exam during which, I was sure, my medical condition would arouse tedium in her all over again.

She wasn't wearing a wedding ring, but that doesn't mean anything these days.

"There's one other thing," she said, looking down at the other sheet of paper. "I just saw a patient who stabbed himself in the leg. He had . . . went a little crazy, but it was predicted."

I ignored her bad grammar. "Predicted?" I asked. "Predicted how?"

"Well," she said, sitting back. "There's this start-up company, Generomics Associates. Bunch of Harvard and MIT graduates, they tell me, mostly in molecular biology and computer science. Genome plus Geronimo, like the Indigenous warrior. They're in Cambridge, the Massachusetts one, across that river from Boston? And they're marketing this blood test, analyzing your genome, DNA and so on. It's somewhat secret, what they're doing. The jury is still out on the science of this thing, but we have . . . I need to tell you that your insurance won't pay for it. It's still somewhat speculative and experimental, this test they've invented." She waited. "I have my doubts about it, myself. If it's what they say it is, whoa. But if you want to pay for it, you can get it. Results come back in two, three weeks."

"So what does it tell you?"

"Well." She smiled, as if she was divulging a secret. "As I said, they take your blood sample, get your entire genome, run it through a supercomputer, and then they digitize it and, you know, they have these algorithms that . . ." Her voice trailed off. "I'm not sure how they do it. I'm just a country doctor. But we have . . . It's been decided that we should tell people about it, in case they want it." She probably meant: the clinic gets a kickback if you agree to this thing.

"But what does the test say?" I asked. "I'm confused."

"It's predictive," she informed me, twiddling a ballpoint pen between her fingers.

"Like what diseases I'm going to get? Hereditary, like that?"

"Yes. Well, and also no. No, not this test." She glanced at the clock on the desk. "It's, I don't know . . . I suppose I should give you the literature. I've got the brochure over there. What it does is, it predicts *behavior*, tells you what you're going to do *before* you do it, based on the . . . *arrangements* in your genetic structure, your psychology, and your past and your what-have-you. Plus your faith history. Plus how you fill out the questionnaire. Plus who knows what. Your internet purchases and browsing history—things like that. With these computers, and the fancy algorithms, and the way you answer their questions and stuff, they can get very specific. There's nothing these mainframes don't know. They can figure out *anybody*. Like that person I was telling you about. They told him he was going to stab himself in the leg, and, guess what, he went and did it. Or so I heard." She stopped twiddling the pen. "Probably it was an accident. Who stabs himself in the leg? Nobody! Anyway, science marches on."

"Pretty specific scientific guess marching on, right?"

"You can say that again," she said, and when she nodded, her glasses hanging on their chain trembled a little. "Anyway, you want this test, totally your decision by the way, we can order it up for you. Results take two or three weeks to come back. Did I say that already? But I should warn you: it's expensive—couple of thousand dollars." She turned away from me and fastened her gaze on the computer screen on her desk. I noticed that she repeated herself, pure absentmindedness on her part, an inability to live in the moment thanks to routine boredom.

"I'll do it," I told her decisively, and she signed the test order sheet before handing it to me. Maybe I should have been more careful, done a bit of research first, but I've always been curious about what I was about to do. Everybody including me says I'm as predictable as a clock. I have had very few problems with impulsive behavior. And addictions? They never had a grip on me. But what the hell. For the two thousand dollars, I could buy this fortune cookie and find out my future and then eat the cookie. What *was* I going to do with what remains of my life? I would have liked to know myself. *Know thyself!* A directive from ancient times. Besides, who doesn't want to know the future?

Call it an impulse purchase.

Someone came in and took a vial of my blood. That was it. That simple. They gave me the questionnaires, etc. Something about all this was fishy, but I was in. I had signed up. There was a dotted line and my name was on it.

2

MY EX-WIFE, CHERYL, LEFT ME TWO YEARS AGO AND RAN OFF WITH A subcontractor. I guess it was the tool belt and the know-how that got to her. They live in a leaky and shabby little house, their love nest. Our kids—Joe, who's fifteen, and Lena, who's seventeen— live here with me most of the time. My kids like me better than they like their mom. Cheryl's the impulsive one. They don't trust her, not even for lunch money. The subcontractor, Burt, is even worse on the impulsive scale than Cheryl is. Don't get me started on Burt. Besides, I'll get to him eventually.

I'm the opposite. I time every domestic event with schedules, so dinner is always on the table at six p.m. thanks to me. I do the laundry, pay the bills, including clothes, go to their games and con- certs. Nearly typical teenagers, they treat me with lighthearted, ironic impatience that verges on contempt but never quite arrives there, me being the provider after all, the only Gibraltar rock in a landscape of sand and broken promises. Talk about predict- able! They know what I'm going to do before I do it. With my ex, Cheryl, the future is and was always up for grabs, starting with five minutes from now. You don't want that in a parent.

My daughter, Lena, has a boyfriend, Pete, a nice enough guy, very useful on small fix-up projects around here. I guess it's ironic that my wife ran off with the subcontractor, and my daughter found a guy who could help me repair doorknobs and leaky faucets. He sleeps over here a lot—okay with me as long as they don't make a lot of sex noise and don't monopolize the upstairs bathroom. My rule: Use effective contraception. Her bedside table is therefore awash with condoms. I don't want any babies around here just now. I have my hands full without a squalling infant in them.

Pete's a sleepwalker. He roams around the house at night in his underwear, or less. We're used to it, mostly.

I guess Pete has a parent, a single mom, but I've only met her a couple of times. She has a name: Roxanne Potter. Over the phone she sounds like that hillbilly MC on *America Needs Talent*. She works at Famous Discount. Officially my daughter's boyfriend is Peter Potter, a name to make you smile.

Joe, Lena, and Pete Potter are at home when I get there, lounging around in that teenage way: Joe's lying on the floor and has got earbuds on and is listening to the Go-Fuck-Yourself-Electrocute-Me-Monster-Death-Metal music he likes, singers screaming as if they're being tasered. I can hear it from here. He's going to blow his eardrums out. He'd like to have that look of blood coming out of his ears. He practices his cheap guitar in the basement in hopes of becoming a rock star god. Lena and Pete are sitting on the sofa together, staring at their iPhones and tapping out messages to their set of friends or maybe to each other. For some reason Pete's still wearing his cross-country sweatpants and is barefoot. The sweat from his T-shirt is staining the sofa. I can smell him from over here. You choose your battles, and this one, sweat stains and body odor, is not Antietam.

Cheryl and I share custody, but Lena and Joe prefer it over here. Lena doesn't look up. "Where were you?" she asks. "You're late."

"Who's the parent here?" I ask. "I was at the clinic."

"What's the matter?"

"My body hurts. Here. And here." I touch the sore spots. "Sciatica and diverticulitis."

"That's too bad," she says without sympathy in that monotone of hers when she's barely paying attention. Her other hand is resting on Pete's leg. Teenagers! They're insatiable.

"What's for dinner?" Joe shouts from the floor, a nest-heap of hair under his head. When was his last haircut? Last year?

"Meatloaf!" I shout back. We often have meatloaf. It's nutritious.

"We had meatloaf last week," he complains through the jackhammer noise coming from his earbuds.

"We're having it again but with turkey this time. Turkey meatloaf. It's nourishing."

"So predictable," my daughter says. "And we're out of ketchup."

"No, I got more. Meatloaf is an all-around food. By the way," I tell them, "speaking of that. I'm having a blood test that will predict the future. I mean, it'll predict everything I'm going to do before I do it. Genomes, and like that."

Pete looks up and Lena's hand falls off his thigh. He sort of smiles. "You're already Mr. Predictable. You don't need a blood test." I knew he'd say that.

"Nevertheless," I say.

"You're as predictable as a metronome," my daughter tells me flatly, as fact. It's not praise, coming from her.

Joe takes out his earbuds. "Predicting the future? Is that science or science fiction?" I guess he heard me after all.

"I don't know. I mean, when it's the future, who cares?" I ask him.

He sits up. "No, Dad, listen. You take that test, they're gonna forecast your, like, future fate. For the next few months or years or whatever. They don't need a crystal ball, especially with you."

He smiles and flicks his hair back. "It's like fortune-telling except they've got a mainframe instead of the Ouija board."

There's a pause, and I'm about to go into the kitchen to start dinner when Lena says, "It'd be fun for you to screw it up."

"What do you mean?" I ask her.

"Well, like, the algorithm tells you that you're going to go to Cancún or wherever, and . . . I don't know, you murder some little skank in Utah instead of going to Cancún. *Surprise!*"

"I'm not going to murder anybody," I tell her. "That's crazy."

"Wait and see. You haven't done it *yet*," she says. "But what if . . . what if the machine says that you're *actually* going to murder somebody, and then you do it, *because you say you couldn't help it*? Because it had been predicted and everything? It was, like, science? You couldn't stop your evil bad side from taking over? Which you don't have, but whatever. You could *grow* an evil side. The prediction was down in print, what you were going to do. Predicted on the readout. *That's* your alibi. You had to do it, because the computer said so. And science is real."

"I have to make dinner," I say. I don't like the direction this conversation is taking.

AT THE CLINIC, THEY GAVE ME THE QUESTIONNAIRE, WHICH WAS QUITE long. My other tests, the conventional nonpredictive ones, are scheduled for next week. After dinner, and once the dishes are washed, I Google Generomics, but nothing comes up. That's very odd. There's nothing about the company anywhere on the internet. They might be entirely bogus! Failing that, I bring the questionnaire into the den and start to fill it out. It takes hours. There are more questions than you can shake a stick at, and it starts out with standard stuff: biography, family, educational history, highlights of my health, my daily habits, my ambitions in life, what are my faiths, what I believe in order to get out of bed in the morning, etc. But toward the end, some of the questions go into a strange place. Here's a sample.

- PLEASE DESCRIBE YOUR LATEST TRAFFIC ACCIDENT. LIST THE INJURIES.
- IF YOU ARE MARRIED, HOW LONG WAS YOUR HONEYMOON?
- DESCRIBE, IN DETAIL, YOUR STRANGEST THOUGHTS. INCLUDE COLORS AND SMELLS.
- HAVE YOU EVER HIT ANYONE IN THE FACE? WHY? (YOUR ANSWER WILL BE KEPT CONFIDENTIAL.)
- HAVE YOU EVER LEFT A ROOM THROUGH A WINDOW, RATHER THAN THE DOOR? EXPLAIN.
- DESCRIBE THE SCARS ON YOUR BODY AND THEIR ORIGIN.
- WHAT IS YOUR PREFERRED METHOD FOR OPENING TIN CANS?
- GRACIELA DID NOT INVITE YOU TO HER BIRTHDAY PARTY. EXPLAIN WHY.
- WHO IS REALLY IN CHARGE?
- WHY ARE MANHOLES CIRCULAR?
- WHEN YOU WERE BORN, HOW OLD WERE YOU ACTUALLY?
- IF YOU BELIEVE THAT HEROES EXIST IN THE PRESENT, NAME ONE.
- WHAT IS THE LAST STOP ON THE F TRAIN? USE YOUR IMAGINATION.
- HAVE YOU EVER MASTURBATED IN PUBLIC? WHERE AND WHY?
- WHAT OTHER HEADS SHOULD BE ON MT. RUSHMORE?
- IF YOU FOUND OUT THAT GOD DOES NOT LIKE YOU, HOW WOULD YOU FIX THE PROBLEM?

This doesn't look like science to me, or a close relative of science, but who doesn't want to know what the future has in store? The big-brained tenured characters who wrote up these questions—high-powered people with doctorates—work at Harvard and MIT in Cambridge, Massachusetts, the IQ capital of North America. They must know *something*. For example, they know how to keep their company off the internet and away from prying eyes. So I doggedly answer each and every question, taking breaks now and then. I check on Joe. Has he done his homework? And Lena and Pete: they're up in her bedroom and they're actually studying. Still barefoot, he's got his head stuck in his biology textbook, and she's reading *Jude the Obscure*. They wave at me as I stand out in the hallway, looking in at them. Those two get lonely without each other. I guess it's really love, teen love, of course, but they make each other happy, so who cares what it is?

Once I finish the questionnaire, still awake, I watch some late-night TV: *Greased Lightning,* that show about the two escapees from a Vegan Techno-Satanic Cult in Arizona, their adventures and how they're running for their lives. It's a little like that old show *The Fugitive,* except in *this* show, genuine licensed hellhounds from Hell are on their trail. The hellhounds have cameras lashed to drones. They're carrying a wormhole of some kind around with them that leads to an alternative universe that looks like a 1940s black-and-white movie. It's a popular show. Everyone feels like a fugitive right now. I recall that a recent poll shows that 54 percent of people in the United States believe in demons with hooves and pitchforks. They await the resurrection of John F. Kennedy, Jr. But I doze off. It's been a long day. When I wake up, I shut off the TV and head upstairs to bed. Joe's asleep, and my daughter and Pete are making nightly love (I can hear them, her soft groans, the headboard knocking rhythmically against the wall, speaking of metronomes), but I pay them no mind. I walk right past their closed door and go into the bathroom to take the antibiotics they gave me at the clinic, and then I proceed to my bedroom and undress and get into my pajamas, and I say my evening prayer for the souls of everyone, living and dead. God is watching over us and is arranging the future that computers can only guess at, and once I'm under the covers, that's it, that's the day.

3

AS TIME GOES BY, I KEEP THINKING ABOUT WHAT LENA SAID ABOUT ME murdering somebody. It isn't just that it's unlikely, given my mild temperament. It's that I can't think of anybody who (whom?) I want to be dead. You can see I worry about proper grammar. People who worry about proper grammar—who, *whom*—don't go around shooting and stabbing and poisoning other people, as a rule.

For example, you take my ex-wife, Cheryl, who you'll remember ran off with the subcontractor. Sometimes in real life, there's high drama with divorces, separations, and adulteries. In the movies, the adulterous couple, caught in bed, are blown away into little Technicolor blood spatters of viscera that stick to the motel wall and the bedsheets. No question of motive there! Jealousy! The green-eyed demon. But let's face facts. Cheryl got bored with me, got bored with domestic life, got bored with housekeeping and raising kids. Boredom: that American problem, and, more personal, a problem for her, with me, Mr. Predictable. Getting a job at our local 7-Eleven as night manager did not solve her issues. Made them worse, in fact, all that nocturnal thinking in the back room while the Slurpee machine ground on as if nothing was happening.

She wanted to breathe the air of other planets.

Poor woman, she went to work at 7-Eleven as an assistant manager to have extra money for Christmas presents and instead she discovered despair under the harsh fluorescent lighting. Falling in love with the subcontractor felt like a solution to the major life problems: the boredom I already mentioned, despair, nothingness, loneliness, soullessness, doubt, God's death, global warming, an accompanying pandemic, and a total indifference about what's for dinner.

To bond herself to her boyfriend, she even joined a sort of cult that the subcontractor was already in. It was called R/Q Dynamics. The R/Q Dyna-mites, as I call them, believe every variety of whoopee. The idea here is that you have to increase your R-power in your life-enhancement complex by taking charge of your decisions and by eating more natural food and meditating. You can start by throwing out anything made of plastic. Plastic is worse than a nuclear reactor having a meltdown. They have a thing about plastic, these R/Qers. According to these initiates, unrecyclable plastic has deadly radiation akin to radon. You'd be better off having forty X-rays than drinking water out of a plastic bottle. When plastic doesn't give you cancer, it gives you physical inertia. You say, "What's the point?" and sit around watching daytime TV thanks to the infinitely small programmed plastic particles that have wormed their way into your bloodstream and your brain. The plastic promotes indifference and apathy and online shopping. Also plastic takes up valuable space in the landfill like corpses in a cemetery.

The R-power is like the life force, only it's invisible, unlike the Q-power, which is active and has a blue aura. You have questions about this? Don't ask me. The mites' Bible is a book, *Unthinkable Things, Unspeakable Truths,* written by their guru, R. Stan Drabble, a charismatic leader who wears a top hat and also plays the trumpet at their meetings. The sequel to that book was *You Have Been Here Before, Mrs. Jones.* I don't claim to understand any of it. It makes no sense to me and never did. I have *not* been here before. But it made sense to Cheryl, who, as an R/Q Dyna-mite, is on Level Two by now, the orange or blue level, I forget which color. She's shooting for Level Four, the red level. You get a ceremonial bathrobe, monogrammed slippers, and this sash-like object, and a little silver-plated pin with R. Stan Drabble's face on it. He's sometimes referred to as "the Commandant." If you're really lucky, you may get to meet the person who claims to be him.

The whole operation is too zany for my taste. On the other hand, if you don't like zany you probably shouldn't live in America. You can always go to somewhere like Switzerland, where you can gaze at the banks, the mountains, and the clocks.

In fact Cheryl called me the other day to ask for money to tide her over. "Hobby, this is the first and last time I'll ask," she said without a trace of guile. She has always called me Hobby, partly because I don't like that nickname. I was on the phone in the kitchen, where I was making chili in a big pot.

"But I'm already sending you alimony," I told her.

"I know, but the roof sprang a leak," she said. "We have to put in a new roof. With roofing, you're talking real money. Economizing on a roof is a fool's errand."

"Whose real money? Mine? Why can't Burt do it?" I asked. "He does that kind of work, right?" I find that I don't like to say the guy's name aloud.

"He tried. He started the job and got up there above the gutters and then lost his balance, and, you know, fell down to Mother Earth from the force of gravity. It's a miracle he didn't break his neck. The bushes broke his fall. He got bruises. Cracked his watch, though. Fortunately, it was just a drugstore timepiece, cheap and inaccurate. Anyway, he wants to get a real roofer in, someone who knows how to do it. That fall wised him up about his limitations."

"He was born under a lucky star," I told her. "The stars and planets coincided in Burt's favor. If I fell off a roof, I'd be dead."

"No, you'd be alive. Don't be so sarcastic. I wish you two could be friends. You have one or two things in common. You're the same age. You've known him since first grade. Are the kids okay?"

"They're fine. You'll see them on Friday. For the weekend," I said, to remind her. Peter Potter, my daughter's live-in boyfriend, did not like my ex-wife and wouldn't go over there (he claimed that she shamelessly flirted with him, which I found unseemly, if true), but he was not welcome here either if Lena was not in the house. He could stay with his single mom, Mrs. Potter. Anyway, my girlfriend, Trey, was going to be here for a while, and I didn't want Pete around when she was here occupying the bathroom, so to speak.

"About that money," she said, steering the conversation back to where she wanted it. "Oh, by the way, I heard that you were taking that blood test that tells you everything you're going to do before you do it." She laughed humorlessly, a sound like throat clearing. "Talk about something you don't need! I can't fathom it. This just beats everything. You sell insurance! When did you ever in your life do anything unexpected? I can't remember a single time you ever took a chance."

"Well, in high school I took you to the prom. How'd you hear about the test?"

"Word gets around. My point is, if you can cough up the money for a blood test like that, you can certainly help out Burt and me, considering the leaky roof and all." She then told me how much she wanted me to fork over to her. It was a substantial figure. What am I, an ATM machine?

"How's your boyfriend's gambling problem?" I asked her. "Has he been making trips again to the Ohio Riverboat Casino and the blackjack table?"

"No. He hasn't done that recently. You were misinformed. He's got it totally under control," she told me. "In fact he's got a gambling addiction mentor named Marvin. He does everything Marvin advises him to do, including that I'm-totally-helpless prayer they all use. Thank goodness for Marvin. Burt's got this gambling thing beat thanks to Marvin and God, which is Burt's Higher Power. He's clean. He doesn't have to make amends. Burt is not an amends type of guy. He's gone back to the gym and these days looks really ripped, like Mr. Muscles. Can I expect that check from you for the roof?"

"It's in the mail as long as it doesn't go for R/Q Dynamics or the blackjack table."

There was a long pause on the other end of the line. "You have my personal guarantee," Cheryl said with angry emphasis. She was hiccuping, I noticed, and the sentence came out with these semi-comic hiccup pauses. Had she been drinking? I wouldn't speculate.

"Okay," I told her.

"We could really use that money," she said. "Oh, I almost forgot to say."

"What?"

"Thank you, Hobby. There," she said, concluding the ask. "We really appreciate it. Thank you ahead of time. I just said it."

"You're welcome."

I SHOULD PROBABLY OFFER A WORD HERE ABOUT THE GIRLFRIEND I'VE taken up with post-divorce. After all, she too is a part of this picture. Some personal matters deserve privacy, but if you're writing up a true account of events, even minor players should get some airtime. And besides, she's not a minor player in her own life. I shouldn't call her my "girlfriend" because like me she's solidly accustomed to middle age.

Her name is Gertrude but everyone calls her either Gertie or Trudy but I call her Trey, my love-name for her. I don't usually describe people, but I'll break my rule here to say that she has a streak of silver in her hair and the kindest eyes you will ever see on a human being. She has a blouse with flower patterns on it that breaks my heart. She's a little plump, but you don't want perfection or towering beauty in a woman because stupendous beauty like that can warp the personality, resulting in vanity, spite, and meanness of the Kardashian variety. This is also true of unpleasantly handsome men like that movie star with the menacing godlike smile. Burt, the subcontractor, is handsome, and I'll get to that eventually. Trey has none of that. She's kind to children, not having any herself, and to animals and plants, flowers in particular. She has glasses with brown frames and wears a junk-jewelry bracelet that when she wears it looks as if it came from Tiffany's.

She works at the Knoblauch County Park as an administrator and a naturalist. She gives tours and nature shows for both schoolchildren and grown-ups. She can imitate owls and has the little kids put their hands through a hole in a box to feel what's inside, a mystery that is eventually revealed. You see a bird in the sky, Trey can identify it by name and habitat. Often she can duplicate its mating cry.

She had a husband once who died in a freak electrical accident. Together in Columbus they worked as contract writers on *The Farm Hour*, a cabaret show on Ohio Public Radio for city folk who sit around drinking martinis while they listen to the host of the show, Benjamin Franklin Shoats, telling made-up stories about farm life, followed by imaginary hog price futures and a march around the barn. *The Farm Hour* also had a polka band staffed by out-of-work symphony musicians from Juilliard. Shoats is as ugly as a gorilla, so it's a good thing he's on radio. The show is a gentle *pastorale* for jaded urbanites. When Trey's husband died in the freak accident—he was barefoot in the basement when he touched an ungrounded Frigidaire—she quit the show, having lost her sense of humor. She went to work outdoors at the county park, where humor wasn't necessary.

Trey's one semi-obsession is saving the planet. This is an admirable ambition that no sane person would criticize. But it has unforeseen consequences. For example, she doesn't want to waste precious water. Okay so far. In practice what this means is that when I go into the bathroom, there is an ambient acrid smell from unflushed urine. Strictly speaking, I'm not complaining here, and as complaints go, this is small and unimportant measured against her almost 100 percent good nature and positive deeds, and besides, we all agree that water shouldn't be wasted with gratuitous flushings of the toilet. She and I met, by the way, at First Faith Free Church, where we were both teaching Sunday school. She had the Old Testament, and I had the New. We've been together for some time now, with the prospect of aging together.

I can imagine many of my possible readers wondering when the trouble will begin in a story told by a "straight" white Sunday school teacher such as myself whose teenaged children complain about how predictable he is. The setting is Kingsboro, Ohio, after all, and not the decaying borough of Queens, New York, or one of the red-light back-alley fleshpots of Reno, Nevada, where there are enticements to every form of vice. What could possibly go wrong in such a place as Kingsboro, even though our small city is a cesspool of pollution, addiction, and potential Superfund sites? And I'm not even discussing our mayor, Mrs. Bonnard Deaver, whose professional ethics are not all that they could be. Nor am I discussing the city council, elected mediocrities who sometimes behave like the clowns at the Shrine Circus. Or the petty criminals who steal hubcaps and cars and get liquored up and go out in public to shout at no one in particular. We've got our addicts and chronically sick characters and hardened evildoers who do not have the law in their hearts. We know them; we know where they are. I'm not talking about those mostly harmless characters.

Have you forgotten about the blood test? The results came back, and I had to make another trip down to the clinic to get them.

4

DRIVING TO THE KINGSBORO MEDICAL CLINIC FROM ALMOST ANY-where, you have to take County Highway 23a. It's an obstacle course of potholes and frost heaves and dead animals picked over by crows, and, I have to say, by the occasional eagle. With my own eyes, I have seen deer, possums, foxes, squirrels, and two raccoons by the side of the road, such animals having met their fate under the tires of crazed motorists who couldn't be bothered to swerve to save a four-legged life. Invariably the animals die with surprised expressions. These critters are polite and shy and emerge at dusk only to be flattened underneath someone's all-season radial tires. I feel sorry for them, though my grief is not excessive.

And don't get me started on highway maintenance here in Knoblauch County. The potholes and frost heaves and the miscellaneous cracks and bumps give any car's shocks a thorough workout. Driving down that road is like sitting in one of those knock-your-teeth-out thrill rides at the Cedar Point amusement park. They shake you up at high speed until you're sick enough to vomit and then they let you go on your way. Alongside the highway you see abandoned cars that couldn't pass muster and died right there on the spot. They have been vandalized, picked over, and are missing their radios and hubcaps.

Still, it was a sunny day when I drove to the Kingsboro Medical Clinic. I was feeling optimistic about my prospects despite the jostling on the road.

I parked my car in the lot as far away from the other vehicles as I could. Actuarial tables will tell you that people who have been given a diagnosis of a terminal illness are reckless drivers, and you should stay away from where they park after they've gotten a diagnosis or at any other time. They have nothing to lose, flinging open the car doors and sitting down without attaching the lap-and-shoulder belt before they apply the heavy foot to the accelerator pedal as they open their fourth can of beer. Read the statistics if you don't believe me. Only Mormons, as a group, are more reckless behind the wheel. I could show you the numbers. I walked in through the double door and observed a sorry example of humanity dressed in an overcoat being wheelchaired in the opposite direction. The golden ager's bald head went up and the rheumy eyes fixed on mine and gave me a baleful glance. A guttural noise came out of the oldster's gaping mouth. I am compelled to say that this individual gave off an unclean smell. Undeterred, I entered the lobby, brushing past a giant plant with horror-movie leaves that groped blindly in my direction.

After an interminable wait during which time I read a six-month-old issue of *Suburban Patio & Swimming Pool* magazine, I was hustled into a consulting room. There was a desk, a blue plastic chair next to the desk, an examining table, a lamp, and another matching blue chair. On the wall was a photograph, meant to calm you down, of a river and trees, but it lacked narcotic effectiveness. On another wall was a poster labeled "The Six Warning Signs of Lung Cancer." The poster had a picture of a young woman, evidently a doctor, complete with stethoscope, smiling outwardly with her index finger pointed straight up as she made her dire point. I had gotten past *persistent cough, rust-colored sputum,* and *difficulty breathing* when someone knocked. I said, "Come in," and in walks a youthful bearded bespectacled fellow wearing a suit under a white smock, and he's carrying a three-ring binder. In his suit coat pocket is a pocket-square hankie that matches his purple amoeba-paisley tie for a dapper effect. We are both wearing face masks, though I have been vaccinated and am Covid-free. He has the abstracted look of someone waiting for Friday so that he can collect his paycheck. In other words, he is not quite here.

He holds out a fist for a fist bump, so I bump his fist. "Mr. Hutson," he says by way of introduction.

"No, I'm sorry, you're mistaken, though it's a common mistake. It's *Hobson*. Brock Hobson."

"Yes," he says. "Apologies. Pardon my blooper. It does say 'Hobson' right here on the top sheet, plain as day." Behind his mask, he gives me a split-second smile, mostly with his eyes. The smile doesn't linger and has no value. If you weren't as attentive as a hawk watching its prey, you'd miss it. "Anyway, I'm here to explain your test results to you. They're quite complicated and need some interpretation. Sorry that I got your name wrong." Still standing and looking down, he's flipping through pages in the three-ring binder. He's wearing a department-store cologne that smells like a spicy swamp.

"Quite all right." I search for his name tag but can't find anything. "And you are?"

"We'll get to that," he tells me. Young professional people like this character today have few of the social niceties, it seems. Introductions? Forget about them. Recreational drugs and medical school arrogance have knocked this guy into the psychic ozone. Given his abrupt and officious manner, he must be yet another MD with a high opinion of his opinions. The arrogance comes with the diploma. He sits down at the desk, opens the binder again, and takes a long look at the first page as he removes his face mask. "Well," he says. He flips two pages over and says, "Well

well well," again, breathing out through his mouth. "Where do I start?" He glances up at me, examines my face as if it were a clue to a future crime, then scrutinizes the page again. I take off my own mask. This anonymous character has no bedside manner to speak of, I'm thinking, when he suddenly closes the binder and says, "I'm the regional representative for your case from Generomics Associates. I'm Doctor Pilensky, but you may call me Al."

"Like the song."

"Excuse me?"

"The Paul Simon song. 'You Can Call Me Al.'"

"Never heard it," he says, irritably shrugging.

"It was a popular song," I say, leaning back. "Top Forty hit. Very upbeat."

"Really?" He's skeptical, as his Generation X or Y or Millennial or whatever letter now his types usually are. We're already in some sort of pissing contest, this Al and me. I don't know why men do this, but we do.

"'Roly-poly little bat-faced girl,'" I quote to him, from the song.

"Ah." He waits and doctors himself up a little, getting huffy. "Shouldn't it be called 'You *May* Call Me Al'?"

"It's quite a good song," I tell him. I'm about to go to my iPhone so I can play it for him when he waves his hand at me.

"I believe you. I just haven't heard it."

"Have you heard 'Mother and Child Reunion'? It's on the same album."

"No. Haven't heard that one either. I *have* heard 'Bridge over Troubled Water.'"

"Well, everybody's heard that one," I say. "Dead people have heard that song. Martians have heard it. That's on a different album."

"I feel," he says, "Mr. Hobson, that you and I have perhaps gotten off on the wrong foot. Or feet. Shall we start again?"

"I couldn't agree more, Doctor Al."

"Perhaps I should get down to business, uh, *Brock*. We have quite a few interesting graphs and charts here. Yours was one of the most unusual genome blood tests and questionnaires that we have ever processed, I can assure you. Everyone in the company— the imagineers, the blue-sky solutioners—had similar reactions to the almost nonsensical data from you. We were initially flummoxed, unable to cross the bridge over the river that flows downward to . . . whatever. Most of the results, however, are quite technical and might not make much sense to a layperson. Which you are. And the results themselves may have a critical valence, like a revolving door, for example, going both in and out, omni-directional. What we need is the pivot on which the revolving door turns. We are not revolutionary but rotational. I will try to avoid technical jargon, however. For example, let me turn to page four."

On page four, he shows me the first "analytic," as he calls it. It's in the form of a graph:

"Note the downward slope?" he asks me, tilting his head back as if I'm a third grader. "Those are your *prospects*, as we call them. The first column represents fifty future-tags, the second column represents twenty-five future-tags, and the third column on the right represents ten future-tags, which I'll define in a moment. When we say 'prospects,' however, we do not *use* the word or *mean* it as *you* might employ it in common discourse. What we mean . . . Well, I could probably explain it by alluding to the view an airplane pilot has out through the windshield—that is, the view of the sky as mollified by the radar screen on the cockpit dashboard. The pilot may or may not see blue sky or clouds—you can't see blue on radar—but the *prospect* comprises the space of what the airplane is about to enter. Imagine for example a flock of birds."

"Wow. That's so profound. So," I say, "you're using the word 'prospect' in the way everybody uses it, right?"

"Yes and no. We enter that discourse by remarking that when we're at the top of the mountain, vista-wise, we have *a good prospect*. Does that have anything to do with the future? It does not. It has to do with the widening construction horizon of what we can see and therefore where we might go. Is this making any endemic sense to you?"

"No."

One of his thick hairy eyebrows goes up, creating in him a displeasing expression of skeptical dismay. "All right, then." As he speaks, I notice that he has a fine head of hair. As my children remind me, I myself am on that downward slope of hair loss, speaking of downward slopes. I am not yet bald, however. "I'll simplify. Let me be more specific," he says. "As you know, the human genome contains within itself certain whiffs of predispositions. This is very complex and hard to explain to people such as yourself, an untrained layperson. In and of itself, no genome can be predictive, of course, but in combination with your personal faith history and your answers to the questionnaire, we can construct a fairly accurate forecast for whomever takes this particular blood test. In the past we have managed an eighty to ninety percent accuracy of predictive outcomes."

"Whoever," I correct him.

"What?"

"You said, 'for whomever takes this particular blood test.' That's incorrect. It's 'whoever.'"

"I believe you're mistaken. 'Whomever' is the object of the preposition 'for.'"

"Nope. Sorry, Doctor. It's a noun clause. The whole clause is the object of the preposition, and 'whoever' is the subject of the noun clause. I may be untrained, but I went to a Catholic school as a kid and was taught grammar by Jesuits, and Jesuits sure know their grammar. For those guys, it's a rock of certainty in a sea of doubt. Also, Jesuits like logic."

"That's a new one," Dr. Pilensky says.

"Not to me or the Jesuits."

"I'm a scientist," he informs me. "Not a grammarian."

"I'm not a grammarian, either. I just sell insurance. But it's my opinion that scientists should know their parts of speech."

"Do you want to know these predictive outcomes or not?"

"Sure."

"I get the feeling that you're toying with me," he says.

"Naw," I tell him. "That's not my style."

"Okay," he says, "look at this." He points to a page where certain dire symbols are spread out in a relatively neat line.

"Each one of these symbols is mathematically arrived at and they're as complex as Chinese ideograms, and," he says, "in the aggregate they tell us what's going to happen to you and what you're going to do in visual-analytic terms."

"Maybe you could spell it out for me," I suggest, looking warily at the skull and the pie chart that he has set out for my inspection.

"Well, for starters, these symbols would be meaningless unless and until you had gone through the process of training that all of us in the company who do these wholesale interfaces such as I'm doing now have gone through ourselves with reference to particular outcome event results," he says, sounding uneasy with the English language, and breathless. "This heart, for example, does not refer to your heart but to particular emotional barrier reefs, a singular algorithm. And here," he says, "is the sheet with the raw data on it. Brace yourself, Mr. Brock."

"Excuse me?"

"You may be shocked by these results."

"Oh, I doubt it," I say. "Hit me with your best shot."

```
Subject has phenological category δδ
leading to express behaviors of a
criminal or outra-legal type, well-
known among dis-ambulatory and self-
injuring and other-injuring phenotypes.
Common traits among such metahominoids
may include "dope" flagellation and
nonstandard enterprise initiatives for
culturally "unbound" behaviors if and
only if express uncertainties within
previously understood parameters are
not followed to the letter. Company
advises further testing qua profiling
as well as "leaning" on procedure i(a)
(4) in instruction manual #3Q, with
addendum 7G to avoid unforeseen, pro-
digiously unfavorable outcomes.
```

"Well, Doctor Al," I say, "I only went to Ohio State. I guess you have to have gone to an exclusive Ivy League school to understand that."

"Unquestionably. Let me simplify it for you, Mr. Bruck, as I indicated." He takes a deep breath. The glasses he's wearing are trending downward on the right side of his face. "It's predicting criminal behavior on your part. Also drug taking and possible anti-social tendencies. But the criminal activity is the one to keep in mind. This suggests felony-level misbehavior. Maybe not electric chair–worthy criminality, okay, and the gas chamber and the firing squad are off the table, ditto the guillotine, but felonies are definitely in your future. Of course we need to take more tests. Several of them." He has an effortless condescension. It costs him nothing.

"Yes, I can see that. But who's this 'we'? My guess is, those tests will cost more money. No doubt I should be on my guard." I'm not convinced by these predictions. They're quite implausible given how upstanding I am. In any police lineup I'd look like a well-fed Rotarian. I don't have that mass murderer smirk. "What sort of criminal behavior? Do you know? Does the computer know? And how come your company isn't on the internet?"

"The particulars of criminality? No, I don't have the specifics on that," Dr. Pilensky says. "All that would be up to you." He coughs once without covering his mouth, reaches into his pocket, and pulls out an orange breath mint. "Criminality is a gray area and is as large as a person's imagination. It's not like we can predict when you'll go to the bathroom. Or when you'll walk Fido. Trivialities are not our style, you see. We deal only with consequential behaviors and the big picture, with about ninety-four percent accuracy. That's the major league ballpark we play in. The biggest of big pictures. So what's certain in your case is, as I said: *criminality*. That's the tobacco in your pipe, which you will be smoking."

"Criminality? Like a murderous rampage? This all seems like a big jump over the line to pure ludicrous speculation to me."

"Au contraire. It's quite scientific. The blue sky is the solution, not the speculation. These giant mainframe computers and the algorithms that they've come up with in Cambridge, Massachusetts, have never been wrong. Tremendous brainpower and hours of research have been applied to these problems by the smartest people imaginable, the best and brightest so to speak. The machines are smarter than we are. Have been, for a long time. The testing procedures have been rigorous. Our AI machines are made in Germany. We have experts with degrees from Yale. We are never wrong, and when someone in our organization *is* wrong, bye-bye to him. Or her. Or them. The test subjects included both people and monkeys and a few lab rats. The machines have staged thousands of real-world real-time enactments. They are brilliant down to the quantum level and are self-replicating. The margin of error is therefore close to nonexistent and perhaps below that."

"Well, then. What can I say? I guess it's time for me to go."

"Very well then. I'll give you the full computer readout." He hands me a stapled set of blue papers about the size and heft of a long essay. "These are the results of the blood test in detail. And we ask that you make another follow-up appointment."

"Does everybody get a prediction of criminal behavior? I'm just asking."

"Oh, no. You're the first to get that. The previous person I talked to seems destined for sainthood. You could almost see the halo forming. We are expecting a miracle or two."

"Wow. I'm impressed. But maybe you got the results reversed. You know: mixed up, me with him."

"Her. The proto-saint. Not him. Anyway, that would be impossible," he says with confident aplomb. "These results predict that you are about to embark on a major crime wave. It's all down on paper. I wish you luck and Godspeed."

5

ON THE WAY HOME, I STOP AT THE LOCAL FAMOUS DISCOUNT, WHERE I need to get a pair of pruning shears for yard work. You go into Famous Discount and are confronted with their hollow-eyed minimum-wage employees, beaten-down wage earners, most of them indifferent to anything that happens in the store. It's a strange world these retail people inhabit. They all have to wear the Famous Discount lime-green smock. On the smock is the name tag. "I'm [Brad or Kayleigh or LaTonya] and *I'm here to save you money!*" The sad truth is that they're there to restock the shelves, keep an occasional eye out for shoplifters, and get high on the loading dock in the back during their breaks. Saving you money is not on their personal agenda. The name tags are insincere. Actually, I don't think they're bothered that much about shoplifting. My ex-wife, Cheryl, has informed me about this. The workers don't own the business and don't have any stake in the matter. You could walk out the doors with almost anything except maybe an ultrahigh-def TV or a Smith & Wesson semiautomatic rifle, and they wouldn't stop you. It would be too much bother. It would interrupt the placid tedium of their day. Near the exit doors you do have to walk through a Shoplifting Detecto-Radar thingy, which only works if the product has been given a magnetic charge and is worth something. Most of the merchandise here at Famous Discount is quite worthless and no one would bother to steal it, much less buy it. Also at the exit a flagrantly bored security person is sitting there in a uniform. For that job they hire former football players for the physical intimidation factor, but those guys love to party and arrive at work with hangovers and are usually contemptuous of real work and have been known to take naps while on company time.

I proceed down the aisles of Famous Discount, passing by toddler wear, folding lawn chairs, vinyl birdbaths, cribs, picture frames, cast-off remaindered straight-to-video DVDs of movies you never heard of (*Party Animal IV, The Life and Death of Chopin, Alien vs. Bimbo, Heaven Is a Windswept Hill, High School Murder Spree II, His Holiness Pope Robot, Holiday in Paraguay, Voodoo Chiropractor!, Reform School Orgy, Chainsaw Vixens, The Man Who Loved Glue*) selling for five dollars apiece. A robot pope? Interesting! The cover shows a robot dressed up in clerical garb with a miter on his "head" and holding a staff with a crucifix. In his other hand, the robot carries a rosary. He has oscilloscopes for eyes. Is this a comedy? Or a tragedy? Somewhere in between? After examining *Voodoo Chiropractor!* starring Christopher Walken, I pick up the robot movie instead, and then I find myself in the house-and-garden section in front of a selection of lawn sprinklers. Over there, to my left, displayed haphazardly, are several gardening and pruning shears, with long sharp blades and wooden handles, just the thing for a high school murder spree. The one I'm looking at in particular sells for $21.95.

Now I am confronted with a puzzle. Should I try to shoplift the pruning shears? Upload them physically and conceal them inside my clothes? The big mainframe computer and the experts in Cambridge, Massachusetts, say that it's a likelihood. I'm wearing a light autumnal jacket. I look around. Is anybody watching? I gaze casually up at the ceiling to see how many video cams are trained on this area. I can't see anything of the sort. No one is watching except maybe God. Does my crime spree begin here?

Standing there, with *His Holiness Pope Robot* in my left hand and the pruning shears in my right hand, I feel something I haven't felt for a long time.

Freedom.

I can do anything I want to. I can go wild. I have a perfect alibi. The mainframe has said so.

Besides, here's the thing. In high school many of my classmates went to all-night binge parties and got shit-faced and smashed up their cars and never apologized, even in the emergency room while under sedation as they were stitched up and put into casts. They were unrepentant. Guilt slid off of them like rainwater off a goose. They came to school in mismatching clothes they had shoplifted. Some of my classmates had sex wherever and whenever they wanted it, and certain girls I knew by name got knocked up and disappeared for a while or found themselves in abortion clinics miles from home. The never-say-die Kingsboro youth-funsters went skinny-dipping or fell into swimming pools with their clothes on and bragged to me about it later, and they got pierced and tatted and dyed their hair blue. They smoked weed and snorted coke and went into their final exams so high that their eyeballs looked like spinning roulette wheels.

Sitting in the back rows of classrooms with dazed, happy expressions on their faces, my contemporaries, the party animals, answered discussion questions in voices so worn down by sex, drugs, and sleeplessness that you'd need closed-captioning to understand them. They thought Napoleon was the brand name of a shoe polish and that the French Revolution occurred a few years ago in Québec. Ignorance was mother's milk to them. For this crowd, work was too much hassle and studying was for losers. They got wasted in every possible way.

But not me. I played by the rules, all the rules, every single rule. Someone had to do the dishes and clean up after everyone else had staggered home or passed out on the lawn. That person, the cleaner-upper, as you may have guessed, was me. I somehow skipped over the fun and the craziness because I thought that Heaven was my destination. My church and my parents had convinced me of that. I believed the advertising. Young people—a group in which as a teenager I did not include myself—were stupid and impulsive by nature. (And so was my hard-drinking mother, but that's another story; I cleaned up after her, too.) So I missed out; after all, winter was coming as was the Final Judgment, and I believed that I would eventually enter through the pearly gates as a little lamb without a spot.

I wasn't timid, but I'm afraid that I feared God a little too much. The partygoers stopped smiling when they saw me, and they nicknamed me Old Man. They believed I was categorically opposed to fun. And to happiness. In our high school yearbook, I was voted the one most likely to become a parole officer.

My youth passed by without my ever having been there, in that country.

I could start it up again now by shoplifting a pair of garden shears.

Still, there is that Old Testament commandment about not stealing. This is counterbalanced, however, by the New Testament commandment about forgiveness of sins, especially for people who can't help themselves. We have secular laws against theft. Criminals have few admirers in the long run, especially toward the end, when they're either let out of the pen and in need of a helping hand or, worst case scenario, are executed by lethal injection. But generally speaking, people don't get too exercised about shoplifting from a giant multinational retail outlet owned by a New York City hedge fund and operated by a cartel of international slime. The blood test says, "Why not?" It says, "It's party time! Here's your youth back on a plate." It says, "This is you."

What does God think? I've never been able to answer that question, though I have a guess. There's that commandment I already mentioned, but that was long ago, almost in prehistory, before the era of finance capital.

I'm more a New Testament guy myself: love and forgiveness are more up my alley. I try to do the right thing. A problem: it has made me predictable. In the spectrum where my friends and children live, predictable is next to contemptible.

Anyway, with God, you have to think big. It's possible that there's more than one universe. There could be as many universes as grains of sand on the beach. If God created all that, would He care about me shoplifting a garden implement from Famous Discount? I think not.

Stealthily I slip the pruning shears under my lightweight autumnal jacket. Am I really doing something wrong? Hard to say but maybe so. It's possible that I am being observed by the overhead video spy antishoplifting apparatus. What if I'm caught? What happens then? I press my right arm against the shears to hold them in place. The tips of the blades push against the jacket so that it looks as if I have a man-breast or sharply protruding chest cancer. Well, it's a risk I'll take. My back pain, my sciatica, seems to have gone away. I walk excitedly toward the checkout area, this time passing by the housewares section, where shining stainless steel toasters and unaffordable espresso machines are for sale. Here and there you see bedraggled customers beaten down by life. They are looking at price tags and thinking about their credit card limits and imminent bankruptcy and possible jail time. Are there still workhouses where you labor by piling up stones and then making walls out of them? No: instead of workhouses, we have homeless encampments where poverty has turned ordinary people into lunatics who shout at the empty sky and dance drunkenly alone in back alleys and sleep in trash cans. Still, my fellow consumers are searching for a gizmo that will give them a brief moment of happiness.

Now for the real test. I approach the checkout desk. At the scanner is a young woman, very tired looking, whose name tag says she is Vernice. Underneath her pandemic face mask, she looks at me with an all-consuming indifference bordering on sleep. Like so many others, she's fed up with capitalism, and yet her hair is in cornrow braids. She's made an effort to look nice. You have to give her credit for that. I too am wearing a face mask. I hand her *His Holiness Pope Robot*. She scans it.

"Anything else?" she asks.

"No." I don't mention the pruning shears that I am shoplifting. No point in creating trouble for myself.

I put my credit card into the reader, and in a moment it tells me to remove the card. The receipt is being printed up.

"I saw that movie," Vernice informs me.

"Is it good?" I ask.

"No. This robot becomes a saint because, like, robots haven't sinned, or whatever. It was made in Poland or maybe Lithuania. It has subtitles. They finally crucify the robot. I forget the rest. Do you want a bag?"

"Thanks, but I don't need one."

Now for the final test: I have to go past the football-player security guard and the detecto-machine, but I am not afraid, and, sure enough, I sail out of the store with my movie and my stolen treasure.

I am feeling pretty good. I haven't felt this good in a long time. Is this how criminals feel? For example that phrase, *The World Is Yours*. Walking to my car, I have a spring in my step. I expected to feel guilt. Where is it? What happened to my conscience? Well, I'll worry about that presently, a word that means "soon" and not "now," as most people mistakenly believe.

6

CRIME IS A SLIPPERY SLOPE.

My girlfriend, Trey, is in the house when I get back. Or, rather, she's out in the backyard, weeding her little vegetable garden. I won't bother her with the Generomics predictions of my behavior until she's ready to come inside. Where are the kids—Joe, Lena, and Pete? Isn't this Joe and Lena's weekend to be with my ex-wife, Cheryl? I hear a noise from upstairs but nothing you could construe as productive activity. Should I make dinner? I go to the kitchen and find a beer in the refrigerator, and then, back in the living room, I pop *His Holiness Pope Robot* into the DVD player.

The first visuals that come on are previews, and the voice, speaking in British-accented English, sounds like a snooty tour guide speaking into his microphone at the front of the bus. The preview of *The Life and Death of Chopin* shows this long-haired guy playing the piano and then coughing and spitting up bright red blood on the ivory keyboard. Then there's a cut, what I think they call a wipe, and we see Chopin kissing a tiaraed aristocratic lady in a drawing room and then he's hacking up goop again and the blood comes out onto his hankie. *Very* sad. The lady is appalled and is crying big tears and exclaiming in French. It's clearly an art house movie full of miserabilium. Then we see Chopin stroking a cat and laughing with his few close friends, and in the next preview scene he's in a concert hall in the middle of a concerto of some kind in front of the orchestra, and they cut to shots of the weeping audience and he's playing away and then, uh-oh, he faints, slumping over the keys before falling to the floor. That's unfortunate. Finally the cast is listed, with Martin Dunkerley in the role of Chopin, Gladys Cox as George Sand, D. Zalk as Berlioz, and "I'm Always Chasing Rainbows" on the soundtrack. I doubt that movies could get much sadder than this one.

Tragic biographies are not my cup of tea. Well, it's only five dollars retail if you buy it at Famous Discount, but as my father often used to say, a thing you don't want is expensive at any price.

Another preview, this time of some creature-from-outer-space movie, though what's interesting this time is that the creature, which is reptilian and has scales, is clearly female and on a rampage. It's not carrying a purse but you can tell. Watching the preview, I can't figure out whether this monster movie is feminist (the monster is powerful) or antifeminist (she's unquestionably a monster). The interesting feature about monsters is that they never seem to relax or take a day off. They're always on the prowl in Monsterville and have an insatiable appetite for destruction. With them rage never goes away. No vacation for these characters! They have only one idea: kill anything that moves. It occurs to me that the alien in *Alien* lays eggs. This leads me to more back-alley thoughts before *His Holiness Pope Robot* flashes up on the screen.

The movie comes to us from Intraglow Studios, and is released courtesy of Salted Ground Associates Ltd. with additional financing from Canal + and The Lundholm Group. In the first scene we see scientists in a laboratory with blinking lights and switches and multiple computer screens. They are assembling a robot, all right, and the plan—I'm drinking my beer and reading the subtitles—is to make an android that will help with your homework or housekeeping or go into toxic environments like melted-down nuclear reactors, but once they put this contraption together, it (and you can tell that there's an actor inside a robot suit) raises its right arm and blesses the scientists and says it was sent from God to redeem humanity. That's an interesting first act of a story, and it's untouched by irony. The robot was not programmed to say that but said it anyway.

The robot has just managed its first miracle—bringing back sight to a near-dead blind homeless guy living under a bridge—when Trey comes in from the garden. She's wearing a T-shirt soiled with garden dirt, and a pair of old jeans. Her hair is pinned back so that it doesn't fall into her pretty brown eyes. My heart does a little love-thump when I see her. She takes off her gardening gloves and says, "Hi, sweetie. What're you watching?" and I start to tell her the title, but she's off to the bathroom to wash her hands and clean up, so I don't have to do a plot summary. When she's back, she sits down and sort of ignores the TV screen (I have muted the sound), and she asks, "How was your day?"

"Interesting," I tell her. "I bought this movie at Famous Discount. And the Generomics people told me what I was going to do. In the future, I mean."

"Oh, really?" she says in a bored way. "Listen, we have to think about dinner."

"Where are the kids? Don't you want to hear the predictions?"

"Well, Peter and Lena are upstairs doing whatever," she tells me, "because Cheryl hasn't picked Lena up yet, and Joe is out somewhere. I think he said he'd be back in a few minutes. Maybe he's already at Cheryl's. That reminds me. We need to talk. Have you said anything to Joe lately?"

"Well, sure. I see him every day. What're you saying? Talk to him about what?"

"Something is going on with him."

"He's fifteen," I point out. "Of course something's going on. Puberty is hitting him in the teeth. And elsewhere."

"No," she says. "It's not that." She waits for a moment. "Please turn that off," she says, pointing at the TV screen, where the robot is now dressed in clerical garb and is raising the dead. The revived dead look pretty bad, gruesome though alive.

"Okay." I turn down the sound.

"I think . . . I think he's very, very unhappy. I'm worried about him."

"He seems cheerful to me," I tell her. "He was kidding me the other day about how predictable I am and all that."

"The thing is, you don't go into his room."

"Why should I go in there?"

"Well, because. I go into his room to clean up sometimes and just sort of check things out. I'm the laundry lady, right? But not his mom? And he has these notes lying around half-hidden and sort of out in the open and folded up as if he wants someone to read them, so I unfold them just to see what he's written, not that I'm spying exactly. I'm not his mom when I do this. I'm just *playing* his mom." She reaches into the pocket of her jeans and pulls out a piece of paper. Slowly she hands it to me. I open it to read it, and it says, "Kids in schools with guns—I get it."

"Jesus" is all I can say.

"And this one." She reaches into another pocket and pulls out another piece of paper. " 'Now more than ever it seems sweet to die.' "

"Isn't that a quotation?" I ask.

"What?"

"That's a quotation from somewhere. I'm sure of it."

"Who cares if it's a quotation? He *wrote* it."

"Well, I know he wrote it or rewrote it but he didn't think it up. Someone else wrote it first. Keats or somebody. I wonder where he read it."

"Brock, honey, this is your *son*. And there's this other message right here. 'It's so fucking hard to exist. I wish I didn't exist.'"

"Maybe he doesn't really think that," I suggest in a quiet voice. Suddenly I have nothing to say, being perplexed. I don't want to sound insensitive, but it's hard to accept that your son may not want to live the life he's been given or any other life, for that matter. You want to fight despair in your child. You don't want children to harm themselves. You don't want your kid to go down that lonesome road of drug taking, followed by poor grades and the occasional overdose. "Do you think he's picking this up from those chat rooms he goes to and what he's reading on the internet?"

"I don't know," Trey says, nervously pushing a stray curl behind her ear while she attempts a smile. I can see dirt from her gardening under her fingernails. "Is that even relevant? Who cares where he's getting this from? He's being cheerful on the outside but this is what he's thinking. And the internet—it's full of adolescent kids talking about suicide, right?"

"Well," I say, "maybe it's standard-issue adolescent flimflam. It could just be that. Teenagers feel despair all the time. Just *look* at them. That's what they do. They despair. Why shouldn't they?"

"I just feel we should tell Cheryl. We should intervene."

"Who?"

"Cheryl. Your ex-wife."

"Oh, right." I give it a moment's thought. I am actually in an emotional black pit just now. "Did I tell you that she's asking me for money? For a roof? Actually I don't think we should tell her just yet. She'll try to make Joe sign up for R/Q Dynamics and all that R. Stan Drabble mysterioso stuff. She'll hook him up to one of their electric coils for shock treatment. When you feel like shit, those people descend on you like flies."

"Well, anything that works, right? I think you need to talk to Joe."

"What do I say?" I am still trying to crawl out of the black pit my son's despair has immediately put me in. The poor kid. Did I do this to him? But I don't let my feelings show on my face or anywhere else.

"You're his father," she tells me as if I didn't know. She's sitting next to me and is giving me a long semi-spousal look in which my deficits and my advantages, my pluses and minuses, are being calculated. You get this sort of human profit-and-loss exam from women before you marry them. They're making a bet on you and they want to know the odds, but after the wedding they don't care that much anymore, at least for a while. All the accounts are temporarily settled.

"Don't you want to hear about what the Generomics people said my future will be?" I ask her.

"No," Trey says. "I'm not interested. I want to make dinner."

"They said I have criminal tendencies and will soon lead a life of crime."

"No kidding. *You?* That's a good one. I'm sorry you spent all that money on the test. It's bogus. What a scam! You couldn't commit a crime even if you had help doing it." She turns around and gives me that appraising glance again. "You really need to talk to Joe."

At the moment, the robot is up in the window of St. Peter's Square gazing down at the huddled Catholic masses cowering in the rain—the shots don't really match—and raising his arm in a robot blessing. I shut off the DVD player and go in search of my son. So far, no one seems particularly interested in my future life as a bad guy. Too bad I don't have a scar on my face and sinister Satanic mottos tattooed on my neck. That'd scare them! The stolen pruning shears are already on the backyard patio, Exhibit A, and now unimportant in relation to everything else. Where's the prosecutor? Nowhere in sight.

7

JOE ISN'T UP IN HIS ROOM, AND I REMEMBER ALL OVER AGAIN THAT it's Friday and the weekend's coming up, and he'll be over at Burt and Cheryl's doing whatever he does over there. I can't very well talk to him about his suicide notes, not with my ex-wife and her boyfriend in the house chiming in, so I decide on a delaying tactic: if I get into my car and go somewhere and then come back, I can claim that I tried to find him. But I actually do want to find him. I need to wait until Sunday, when I retrieve him again.

My car starts right up as if it wants an adventure, and I head into downtown Kingsboro, passing the hotel designed by Frank Lloyd Wright or someone Prairie School like him. You go in, bending a little for the low ceilings, and suddenly it's 1922 and everything is up-to-date to that year including electric lights and leaded glass windows. I pass the town square and the cannon commemorating the veterans of the GAR and the standing soldier signifying our numerous foreign wars, and then I pass by the now vacant Glass Block V Store and the Who's Hungry Now Café and the sport-and-tackle shop, All Outdoors. I park the car and walk over to the town square and sit down on one of the benches.

Why can't people be happier than they are? Why all this discontent? Why must our children suffer? I'm not philosophical but even so I don't understand anything. A few birds are flying around overhead, and I look up at the blue sky to see where they're going.

They aren't going anywhere in particular. Birds are impulsive and whimsical. I seem to have talked myself into stealing a pair of garden shears from a discount store, and now my son is broadcasting his suicidal unhappiness to anyone who picks up his notes in the house. In front of me is a statue of Charles King, founder and first mayor of Kingsboro. It's been defaced, this statue: someone has painted his hair bright orange and drawn a big red killer clown grin on his face, and there are more hideous spots of yellow paint in and around his crotch area, signifying a genital emergency. Right now I don't know where to find Joe, but I can't really go over to Cheryl's place. I am stymied. Overhead, even with all those birds in it flying back and forth, twilight is threatening us.

I can feel my eyes watering out of sheer unhappiness. Another question: Why can't our lives be simple, like the one that Thoreau led in a shack on Walden Pond? Well, the mad bomber and social theorist Ted Kaczynski lived a simple life in a shack too, before he was hauled away to prison, where he died, so maybe that's not the answer. Why does unhappiness always have to strike so close to home? Why are the teen years so hard to live through for the kindhearted? My head is a ticker tape of ultimate questions going unanswered.

On the bench set in concrete and perpendicular to mine there's a gentleman vagrant wearing a uniform: one of those standard-issue stained overcoats that those characters wear, rain or shine, and lower down on his torso are the threadbare trousers, and then the blue argyle socks—at least he's wearing socks—above the shoes with semi-tied laces, and completing the picture back up on his face is the two-day growth of beard below the rheumy eyes and around the open mouth to reveal unsightly yellow teeth. He has neglected his oral hygiene. He's enjoying the stub of an unfiltered cigarette that he probably picked up from the pavement somewhere. My heart goes out to him. I can't help it. He was once someone's baby boy. All the same, I can tell that he's about to unload on me.

"Evening, friend," the man says to me. "I must lay my cards on the table. I am running for governor of the great state of Ohio."

"Good evening." I wait for a moment and express no surprise about his political ambitions.

"We are lucky," he says, "to amble about in the evening air. Do you enjoy free air?"

Is he speaking words that I can't understand, or is this his typical form of speech? There is no way to answer that particular question. It's true that I don't always hear properly.

"I'm sorry," I say, "but I didn't make out that last part. Free air?"

"Let him with ears, let him hear," he says cryptically. Uh-oh: he's rising to his feet and is approaching me. He motions in the direction of the bench on which I am sitting. "May I ease myself down? Are you friend or foe?" he asks. "Friend, I think."

"Be my guest," I say.

"I can tell you're unhappy," he asserts, as he lowers himself to my right on the bench, "from the look on your sorrowful face. I am rather an expert at reading faces. But I am no charlatan. I know you halfway." He gives off a smell of some kind. I can't quite pinpoint it. We're both maskless.

"At what? Reading people? Well," I tell him, "maybe I *am* unhappy."

"And I know *why* you're unhappy." He coughs violently, and I turn away from him. "I've got the second sight. I know many things despite my erudition."

"Yes?" I say. "And why is that?"

"I'll explain. But first, could I have a moment of your time to inform you of an urgent matter concerning the late Queen of England's younger brother? The British Royal Family is worthy of our attention. Might I impose for a mere moment? Do I have your attention?"

"The Queen of England didn't have a younger brother."

"I beg to differ. Yours is a very common misconception," he says. "But the facts are otherwise. The average citizen professes not to know or to care about the late Queen of England's younger brother, who still lives in assisted care. If the truth got out about that fellow, the world would stop spinning on its axis, I can guarantee. The planet would fall into the sun out of sheer disbelief. There'd be incredulity. Weak minds would be driven insane. Cities would be set afire. You would hear screaming."

"I sometimes hear it anyway. So what does this brother have to do with me?" I ask.

"Typical question. Have you not paid attention to the national debt?"

"Not this week, I haven't," I tell him.

"You should."

"What?"

"You should. Do you need a hearing aid?"

"I don't follow."

"Let me explain," the fellow says, folding his hands together. He speaks softly, as a person does when imparting secret information. "The British Royal Family has terrorist connections. It's documented. For years they've organized and operated a worldwide drug-and-torture operation in the wilds of Mexico and the Caribbean English-speaking territories such as Turks and Caicos. Their activities also include brain laundering. Heard of it? I would be doubtful. That's the stage that follows brainwashing and total cognitive wipeouts resulting in imbecility of the kind you see on nightly network television, those quiz shows where no one knows the answer to anything, even the location of Fort Knox and

Grant's Tomb. The British Royal Family's bank accounts are in the trillions of dollars. The crown jewels are the tip of the iceberg, mere show-and-tell cardboard stage props for the benefit of the man on the street. The real money goes elsewhere. Those British royals bought and now own Antarctica. They're going to mine cadmium down there using child labor. It's too cold for machinery, so the royals resort to the kiddies. An Anglo gulag, no conscience about it at all. Imagine: ill fed and poorly shod orphaned toddlers wearing rags digging into the permafrost. Penguins observe them. A tragedy of major proportions! Henry Kissinger is involved, as you can certainly guess. *There's* a man with his pudgy fingers in many pies! A friend of the *entire* royal family! When he dies, he won't be technically dead, per se. Actually he's dead now but is cleverly playing possum. The only public-thinking person who was on to the truly frightful secret menace of which I speak was Lyndon Roche, the one man who could have saved us, a great human being and a genius to boot. If you went in search of one honest person, you would find him. You should read his book entitled *No Such Thing as the Future.* He died in 2019 at the age of ninety-six of causes that are still unknown even though he might have lived easily to the age of one hundred and five or one hundred and six and maybe a decade more if he hadn't been interfered with. No hidden agendas with him. I am proud to be a Rocheite. I could lend you his book. The dust jacket alone goes for thousands among the cognoscenti. The news media distorted Lyn Roche's opinions *every time* that he ran for president of the United States, particularly when he was incarcerated in prison and therefore muzzled by state and federal law.

"Roche exposed Queen Elizabeth's younger brother, Marshall, who was known to drink martinis through a child's straw to show his oligarchical contempt for good manners and *hoi polloi*. Note that I do not say 'the *hoi polloi*,' a usage that reveals the speaker's ignorance of Greek. Back to Marshall. The man ate mashed potatoes without utensils! Lowered his face to the plate. Just stuffed the spuds into his mouth any which way. Imagine the mess. Indentured servants cleaned it up. It's in the record. He snorted so much cocaine that he had only one gigantic nostril in a face pockmarked by disease. Two nostrils fused into one, and from the effect of drug-induced mania his eyes stared sideways like those of a trout. Nothing but babble and slurping sounds came out of his mouth. Rule, Britannia? I beg to differ. These days, he's completely gaga and like his brothers and sisters in dementia he drools. He can't put on his own cuff links. No wonder they don't show the guy in public. Children would scream and adults would cringe and quail. The rising national debt has everything to do with the British Royal Family and its criminal indulgence in senility and swank. If you drain money away as they do, the remaining money inflates like a party balloon."

"Apparently, you are given to speechifying."

"You shall not find me among that sorry company of losers who advocate a foolish brevity."

"So it seems."

"I merely tell the truth. I have two PhDs from Wayne State University but no job. Free education is my mission. I spread the truth at will. *La vérité* in all its complexity takes nature's own time, aeons really, to reveal itself. I *should* be a governor, of something. The polis would benefit from my administration. Sometimes the truth is askew, so I straighten it out. Not incidentally, God does not employ short sentences." The gentleman-scholar coughs with self-assurance.

"You don't say."

"I do say."

"What about 'Thou shalt not commit adultery'?"

"What about it?"

"God said it. It's a short sentence."

"That is one opinion," the vagrant informs me. "There are other opinions."

"It's an Old Testament opinion. It carries weight. What does this have to do with me?" I ask.

"I'm glad you asked me that question. You pay taxes?"

"Of course. Who doesn't?"

"I do not. I have no income. That's by choice. Yet I want for nothing. Ignoramuses pay taxes. And tax revenue gets siphoned out of the country and ends up in the hands of the British Royal Family, those fucking Windsors. Bunch of cocksuckers, you ask me."

"No need to be impolite. No need to use that kind of language. Your obscenity offends me."

"What ails you?" he asks. "I've just told you everything a person needs to know to advance himself in the world. I've offered to lend you a book, *a first edition*. You've offered me nothing except a complaint about obscenity."

"Okay," I say. "I'll tell you. For starters, my son, Joe, is very unhappy. I've had my future predicted by a company in Cambridge, Massachusetts, and they claim that criminality lies in my times to come. Plus which, the world is going to hell." I reach into my pocket, find my wallet, and take out a five-dollar bill, which I hand to him.

"I shall not refuse your very limited offer of charity," he says, pocketing my fiver after examining it. "Here's some advice: Son, the world has *always* gone to hell. Need I remind you that I am running for governor? And yet here we are, breathing free air and sitting in the public square of Kingsboro, Ohio, as the day darkens toward evening, and you have a problem on your hands that is so easily solved that I am confounded that the solution has not occurred to you."

"What's your name?" I ask.

"What's yours?" he asks me suspiciously, as if I were trying to trick him.

"Brock Hobson," I tell him. A pigeon lands on the statuesque head of Charles King and looks down toward me.

"Brock Hobson? That sounds like a made-up name," he says.

"Every name is made up by a person's parents. What's yours? And what's your solution?"

"My name is George. Actually Doctor George B. Graham the Third, at your service." He straightens up to project a form of dignity. "That's a real name. It's not made up. And here's what you must do for yourself and your son and your life. I have the formula."

"What?"

"Ask him what no one else will ask him. Ask him what he wants."

8

AFTER A DECENT INTERVAL, I LEAVE DR. GEORGE B. GRAHAM III, PHD, on his park bench and return to search for my son. I decide to go over to my ex-wife's house, the place with the bad roof. Burt, her boyfriend, the handyman, is bound to be there, and so I have to prepare myself for Burt's disquisitions about deer hunting, R. Stan Drabble's R/Q Dynamics, and those heroic characters, the Navy SEALs. I've got nothing against Navy SEALs except when Burt is talking about them.

I am also thinking of Dr. Graham's advice to me, advice that's crazy but plausible.

Heading over to Burt and Cheryl's little house, I turn down York Avenue, where there's a canopy of oak and maple trees, and up ahead, on the right side of the street, under a streetlight, I see some leaves drifting down in a lackadaisical manner onto the sidewalks. It's the time of day when the sun is deciding whether to set, and when I see a corpse ambling over there, accompanied by a skeleton and a superhero, I remember that tonight is Halloween and spirits are abroad, so to speak. This evening is a ritual spook-fest, but I should be excused for my absentmindedness about what day it is because my kids aren't really children anymore, though Joe used to love trick-or-treating and would dress up in memorable ways: once with slicked-back hair and a pencil mustache and a Bible (a televangelist shill); another time wearing a mortarboard, a coat with elbow patches, a grade book in one hand, and an empty bottle of whiskey in the other (college professor); and, now that I think about it, he later dressed up as an apocalyptician with bloody wrists and kohl-darkened eyes. That one was truly scary. At each doorway, in exchange for candy bars or gumdrops, he gave out a death manifesto that he had written and printed up himself from his computer. Its headline read, "The world would be better off without anybody, including you. And that day is coming on September thirty-first."

But now, after I park the car, I sit back for a moment to watch the parade of disguises. Little girls dressed up in gauzy princess attire walk hand in hand with their parents, who are costumed as themselves—mere tired citizens—although one father holding his daughter's hand wears a Catholic priest's vestments, giving him a child-molesting vibe. A little Darth Vader, carrying a bucket with candy, walks next to a diminutive short-haired girl (I think she's a girl) who looks very much like Harry Potter, and next to them is a very plausible teenaged Spider-man hopping around, a gymnast, almost weightless. Here and there among the heroes and villains and unicorns walk a few ghosts. Someone is carrying a sign, MARTIANS, GO HOME! A little Hulk walks beside a toddling Wolverine. Where's Thor? Over there, near the bushes, is a pint-sized Santa Claus.

The corpse that I saw a few minutes ago is now lying on the sidewalk over there like a real corpse. The children walk around him. I hear one girl cry out, "Oh, I guess he must be dead," and then she walks on past the body down the sidewalk.

It occurs to me—I'm not sure how or why—that maybe the person lying on the sidewalk is actually and newly dead. It could happen. And this thought leads to another one: the Mexicans, our fine neighbors to the south, are quite sensible about death or, as they might think about it, Death, a sort of skeletal character with a capital "D." Death is a member of the family in Mexico, a close relative. They devote an entire day, the Day of the Dead, November 1, to its celebration. Americans would rather sweep death under the rug than celebrate it, a clear mistake. You don't want Death to be the uninvited guest at the end of your life but someone (or something) you've hung around with for many of your adult years and gotten used to. We have Memorial Day, of course, which is not celebratory, but a Protestant chore: flowers, twenty-one-gun salutes, prayers, silence. No fun there. In Mexico, Death is a partygoer. Death greets you at the door and hands you a drink. Maybe it's poison but so what? Forget gloom. Break out the pinwheels, the tequila, the brass band, and the casket.

Why am I thinking about the Day of the Dead instead of the actual possibly dead guy across the street from me? I should help him. It's a failure of go-get-'em empathy on my part, I guess.

I get out of my car and walk over to where he's laid out. The corpse has not moved, and it makes no sound. Either this character is an expert pretender, or Death has actually caught up with him and tagged him. As I approach the body, children and adults get out of my way, but once I am close enough to him—it—I see that the body on the ground is that of one of my clients, Edward Ratner, who has a homeowner's umbrella policy and car insurance through my agency. No life insurance, though! A nice enough guy, an electrician, with what they used to call chiseled features. As I recall, he once played for the Kingsboro High School football team, the Screaming Eagles. A star linebacker, if memory serves, known as the "brick wall," although I may be mistaken about that. But now the brick wall is lying down, flattened.

By the time I get to him, he has attracted a crowd, and one adult is bent over him, pounding his chest and breathing into his mouth. Will Ed Ratner be resuscitated? From a distance comes the hee-haw of an ambulance making its way toward us. Gazing down, I see that Ed has stubble, is wearing a pair of glasses, and sports a relatively clean white shirt and jeans. He still has a strong jaw, for all the good it will do him now. The only way that you'd know he was a corpse *before* he fell down is that he was wearing a set of vampire teeth that the Good Samaritan has removed, and his face is painted chalk white, a death indicator. What's he doing out here? He must have been accompanying some kids, but I don't see his children anywhere nearby. Maybe they ran away to get help. Maybe they were actually scared as opposed to pseudoscared.

The crowd is milling around, and there, off to my right, is Joe, my son, wearing a straw hat and overalls, farmer getup, and he's got his skateboard in one hand and his iPhone in the other. I catch his glance, and he gives back a quick, quizzical nod, as if he's not sure what I'm doing out here, or what he's doing here, either. He's carrying a tin pail for handouts, which he's too old for. Teens like to go out on Halloween to create mischief. Making my way over toward Ed Ratner, I elbow people aside and touch him, whereupon his eyes open as if he's been brought back to life. One woman in the crowd says, "He's resurrected!" I hear the approaching siren before I see the vehicle, but within seconds Ed Ratner is surrounded by EMTs, who have pushed away the rubberneckers and the resuscitation worker and are restoring the recent corpse. A gurney has been lowered, and they've injected Ed with life-giving adrenaline (but his life is my doing: I have brought him back to life) and put a respirator mask over his nose and mouth. Joe watches closely, and before you know it, Ed Ratner sits up a little, back from the dead and the visions of the afterlife, including moving toward the light—inadvisable according to the Tibetan Book of the Dead—and eternal judgment and the Heaven and Hell options (unless all he did was pass out), and they load him into the ambulance and speed him off to emergency care. That's that.

The crowd disperses as the kids go on their merry way, and I head toward Joe, who seems to have lost interest in trick-or-treating.

He's staring vacantly down the street as if a parade of floats and baton twirlers wearing short skirts might suddenly appear. When I approach him, he looks at me with something like apathy.

"Did you do that?" he asks me.

"No 'hello'? No 'Hi, Dad'? No pleasantries?"

"Not this time, I guess," he says, looking less and less like a farmer and more like a kid dressed up in farmer clothes. "What are you doing here? Did you try to kill that guy? Or resurrect him?"

"Um, no. What makes you think so?"

"That blood test you took. I figure it gives you permission to do, like, anything. Right?"

"Where did you hear that? I only got the test results a little while ago."

"I'm just guessing. So you didn't murder that guy or anything?"

"Nope. Not this time. Not ever. Besides, he's a client of mine. It's not smart to murder your customers. Cuts down on the commissions."

"Maybe soon, your life of crime? Anyway, that guy. So you didn't do *anything* to him?"

"Of course not. Why would I?"

"Oh, just for the hell of it. I mean, if Clark Kent could turn into Superman, you can turn into a homicidal maniac. Anyone could. I'm not, like, saying you *did*. Watch the news. Ordinary people blow their fuses and start shooting strangers. So why are you here?"

"I was looking for you."

"Why?"

"My car's over there." I point to where it's parked. "Let me drive you to your mom and Burt's house."

"I've got my skateboard."

"Joe, please. We need to talk. Then I'll take you to Burt and your mom's."

"Oh," he says. "All right."

He loads his skateboard into the backseat and I get behind the wheel while he galumphs into the passenger side and attaches his lap-and-shoulder belt. When I look over at him, I see that he has an expression on his face of impatient teen despair, a first cousin to exasperation, and I think, *the poor kid*. It's hard to know where to drive when you're just trying to fill up the time to talk, so I point the car toward the county park, where the Sidenberg River— it's really not much more than a creek—flows down toward Lake Keating, polluted now with mud, algae, and leeches.

I stop the car in the parking lot, and in the near dark, I get out and sit down on the car's left front fender so that I can soak up the atmosphere. Halloween used to be the gate between late fall and early winter, but with global warming, predictable weather has become unpredictable, and you might as well give up anticipating any meteorological events whatsoever. You can hear the gurgling of the river in front of us, and over there in the picnic area, some other teenagers and young adults have started a sort of campfire and are drinking beer and smoking dope. The skunky odor wafts its way toward us. No doubt they're also doing edibles and shrooms and losing their minds in the general universal love. One of the girls laughs, a laugh like a throttled scream, as if she's having visions.

And the fireflies! In October! Impossible but true. They're coming out of the woods and are dotting the air with their fitful luminescence. They're accompanied by the sound of crickets and the shouts of the stoner partygoers in the near distance. Joe has come out with me and is sitting on the right front fender. We're both gazing off into the distance. This is the only way fathers and sons can talk to each other: if they're looking at something together, over there.

"I remember a story about fireflies," I tell Joe. "My father told me this story. I guess his father must have told him. It's kind of a bedtime story. I haven't thought of it for years. In the story, this girl and boy—I guess they're siblings—escape from a burning house and flee into the woods, pursued by the ogre with no face and three legs, a monster in the shape of a walking slug. The monster has no eyes, but it feels its way forward. That was the part of the story that always scared me.

"The two brave children run deeper into the forest, and the trees regard them impassively. The trees have seen children before, running away from witches and wizards, dragons, and men intent on being murderers. The trees have seen it all.

"Night is falling. The three-legged ogre has given up and crawled back into its lair. But now the children are very deep in the woods, and they are lost. There is no path toward home. Like Hansel and Gretel, who left a trail of bread crumbs that the birds ate, they don't know where they are. Then at twilight, the fireflies begin to appear. Somehow the children know that the fireflies will lead them to safety. Each firefly has a tiny light that appears briefly, on and off, like an airy floating point of light.

"In the story, the fireflies are like guardian angels, and the tale ends when the children are safe, led to the old woodcutter's cabin, where they each have a bowl of porridge for dinner. The next morning, they find their way to the village, where the mayor praises them."

"That's the story?" Joe asks. "They eat *porridge*?"

"Yes, that's it. The porridge is part of the story."

"Jeez, Dad, it's total bullshit. You *liked* that? Even as a story for kids, it's bullshit."

"Why d'you say that?"

"Because . . . the children, I don't know, they're . . . because nobody ever gets saved. Not really. Nobody's *ever* saved." He waits. "My opinion? They don't get out of the burning house, for starters. If they do, the ogre *eats* them. If they get into the woods, they get . . . I don't know, they get, um, lost, and they starve. The birds swoop down on them and, like, you know, *vultures* peck out their eyes and stuff. Anyway, even if they don't get lost, the woodcutter is probably a pervert and rapes the girl. Maybe he rapes her brother too, icing on the cake. That's the reality. That's how it goes, these days. We're living in contemporary times."

My cellphone rings but I ignore it. "Well," I tell him, "life doesn't have to be like that."

"Yes, it does," Joe says, "because it totally *is* like that."

I take a deep breath. Being fifteen years old was never easy and certainly isn't now. "Trey says you're leaving notes in your room and around the house."

"Yeah, well," Joe says, looking down at his hands. We can still hear the orgasmic laughs of the partygoers, a vicious madcap counterpoint to my son's glum mood.

"They're kinda like suicide notes, she says."

"Well, they aren't," Joe says. "Just kidding, you know? But, I don't know . . . a little, like this little portion of them, maybe ten percent? Or less? Trying something out. Maybe that part is true. Or could be. You shouldn't worry about me, Dad. Unless you want to. If you want to worry about me, you can do that."

"How come you're feeling this way?"

"Have you ever been over to Mom and Burt's? Have you even talked to Burt?"

"Well, not recently, no. Not as in 'a conversation,' I haven't talked to him."

"Come back Sunday and take me out somewhere," my son says. "And maybe I'll tell you."

9

I HAVE MENTIONED THAT MY EX-WIFE'S CURRENT BOYFRIEND, BURT, IS a fan of the Navy SEALs, the Ohio State Buckeyes, R/Q Dynamics, bodybuilding, and deer hunting bow-and-arrow style à la Ted Nugent, which is not the sign of a high serviceable IQ. I have also noted that he once fell off a roof, another telltale clue to his behavior. Here's a fuller picture, but note: you can skip over the following description if you know people like Burt, a guy who fits quite comfortably into the Mr. Asshole category. Just flip ahead a couple of pages after you've gone out to your kitchen for some popcorn and a beer, and the story will resume. Just to be fair, I should mention that I don't like him at all and I find him somewhat repulsive. His full name, for the record, is Burtram Kindlov, a cruel misnomer. No kind love from him!

Have you ever been in the passing lane, gaining on another car but still at the speed limit, and someone comes up behind you in a pickup, tailgating three feet behind you, blinking his headlights and honking? That would be Burt or someone of the Burt-type.

Of course my ex-wife is with him now, so I'm not inclined to be gracious. She traded me in for him, smitten as she was, going all in and forgetting about the ninety-day warranty. Cheryl was always an impulse buyer. She proposed to me after our third date.

People talk these days about "toxic masculinity" and "testosterone poisoning," a category from which I consider myself to be exempt, but Burt has apparently been schooled by the Marlboro Man—Marlboro is his brand of cigarettes, and he goes around smelling of rank tobacco smoke mixed with the usual odor he gives off. He has an old Ford F-150 that he doesn't ever wash, while Cheryl drives a rusting Datsun. He goes maskless everywhere, claims to be resistant to all diseases because he drinks chaga tea sourced from mushrooms clinging to birch trees in Minnesota, and he listens to those nincompoops on the radio who spout off about evil liberals and licensed medical doctors. Needless to say, he's also glued to the subterranean regions of the internet where he fills his mind with conspiracy cobwebs and other Mad Explanations, that endlessly renewable insanity. R. Stan Drabble is one spider spinning webs among many other busy spiders. Nevertheless, Burt has an imperturbable ignorance about the world and what people are really like. If you were to ask him where Italy is located on the globe, he wouldn't know but would despise you for asking. Did I mention his hat? No. But you can imagine the hat. I don't have to explain everything.

Given his intermittent employment, his carelessness, his mean streak, and his bad habits, Burt would be no prize to anybody, but here I have to be truthful and submit an important detail about him, which is that by any standard, he is exceptionally handsome. A prank of fate. I've known him since grade school—I've followed his career, such as it is. We're the same age. Full disclosure compels me to admit he's painfully good-looking, and despite the cigarette smoking, he has kept himself in shape, so that from high school onward he has had no trouble attracting girls and had no trouble attracting my ex-wife. He has the wide shoulders, the thick hands, etc. He was a wrestler in high school and acquired the signature cauliflower ears, but despite his unsightly ears, he has never been at a loss for female companionship—women habitually notice him and his deep voice and his cowboy musculature after he enters a room. You can demonstrate good manners to women and talk to them about the novels of Emily Brontë all you want, but even some of the educated ones will flip out when Burt is around. Flagrant male beauty gets their attention. They excuse themselves from your mild-mannered presence and soon are standing next to him, touching him on the arm, smiling and laughing. I don't want to be crude, but you can see that look in their eyes: they want to fuck him without any apologies. It's an animal reaction. Some women, the better ones, are exempt. Cheryl, however, was not.

And so they fall into bed with Burt, and then what happens? If you're a guy, having any woman you want degrades your character. The whole idea of monogamy stops making sense. You treat yourself to just anybody. This leads to lying and subterfuge. The worst part is that you don't have to make an effort to look nice, to be charming, to remember birthdays, to give presents and other tokens of affection. A handsome face and the muscles and the big dick are the passports to everywhere. That passport doesn't expire until you're middle-aged. Anyway, once you have the passport, you grow slovenly. You don't have to write down their phone numbers because they'll call you. The art of conversation? Forget it. You don't need that. A few pleasantries, a ride around town in the truck, a stop at the Dairy Queen, and "Wanna fuck?" will do fine. You sit in the kitchen—Burt does this—and you eat the banana or the orange and throw the peel in the direction of the garbage, and if you don't sink it, you leave the peel right there on the floor for others to pick up. Beer bottles and discarded protein shakes litter the house. A butter plate sits on top of the piano keys. The refrigerator door stays open for minutes at a time. The kitchen becomes a playground for mice. Even the flies in the house are coated with dust.

What I'm saying is, some women have a weakness for such

characters. Guys like this don't get married unless they absolutely have to. They may get cornered into it by a random pregnancy, but these days that stratagem rarely works. Occasionally Cupid's arrow hits a Burt-type, but when that happens, it's one for Ripley's. Most of these men are as vain as beauty contest winners, and they spend hours in the gym when they're not drinking Muscle Milk or watching TV openmouthed or cruising the internet or playing video games or are out in the woods killing innocent-bystander animals. R/Q Dynamics have (has?) taught Burt to take some responsibility for his actions, but he hasn't made it up to full responsibility level yet, what they call "open-throttle individual-ism" enacted by people called "Autonomous Falcons." These are falcons freed from their handlers, a.k.a. government bureaucrats and ordinary day-to-day authorities like the employees at the Department of Motor Vehicles. I used to wonder what Cheryl actually thought about having a faithless guy who does not love her sharing her bed every night, but all she ever said in explanation was "He's a beast, and I want to tame him."

Except for the gym and the hunting, Burt is lazy and empty-headed. He's quite at home here in America, if I could generalize for a moment.

TIME TO RETURN FROM THE LOBBY WITH YOUR POPCORN. HERE'S where the story starts up again. Late Sunday afternoon I pick up Joe at Burt and Cheryl's. My daughter, Lena, has already left with Pete and both of them are back at my house by now. Joe has a hangdog expression as he leaves Burt and Cheryl's house and gets into my car, throwing his backpack onto the backseat floor. His long, embittered hair is flying around.

I need a place to take him where he'll be slightly distracted, somewhere he'll be at ease. So I drive over with him to Famous

Discount, claiming that I want another movie from the bin where I fished out *His Holiness Pope Robot*. On the way, Joe claims that if I really wanted to see another lousy five-dollar retail movie, he could find it for free on the web and steal it, but I tell him that I am a believer in royalties and the just monetary reward of artistic labor. He nods sadly at my tragicomic antique views. "Next you're going to be defending copyright laws," he says to me in the car. "And phonograph records."

Inside Famous Discount, past the snoozing security guard, we make our way down an aisle where a seasonal display of loose-toothed lawn rakes has been set up near housewares. The housewares include a collection of dented Beulah-brand baby humidifiers, and next to the humidifiers are stacks of Ol' Farmhouse cola, which tastes even worse than Polar Bear Club cola, which I once thought was the prizewinner for pure cheap nonstandard refreshment, with its strong flavor of sweetened licorice with hints of garlic. But Ol' Farmhouse takes the cake, the cake in question having an almondy cyanide aroma. They also have a diet cola for the calorie-conscious that tastes like fizzy sugared cat food. On the side of the Ol' Farmhouse bottle is a picture of the eponymous farmhouse, still standing despite what I imagine are the enraged townspeople cheated out of their hard-earned cash that they've spent on this swill in hopes of a moment's liquid pick-me-up.

I am chuckling and in truth have become distracted from my son's palpable misery. He's over there, gazing down at some power tools and lawn mowers on display next to clay flowerpots arranged with no particular pattern or logic. Famous Discount is set up like a treasure hunt or a yard sale. Confusion reigns on the sales floor. You want it, you have to find it. The commodities seem to have been laid out by stoned half-wits. The drugged employees have no idea where anything is. Given all the disarray, shoppers at Famous

Discount can feel the store's contempt for them. If they respected their customers, they'd sort this shit out. But no: it's a labyrinth with expired protein bars at the center.

Needing a task, I grab a bottle of Ol' Farmhouse cola and go over to where Joe is surveying some gardening shears, and I am reminded that this is the part of the store where, a few days ago, I did some practice shoplifting.

"What are we doing here?" Joe asks me.

"Well, I had something to find and buy in here," I tell him. "I'm sure of it. I've just forgotten what it was."

"That's kinda typical of you," he says unmaliciously. He's smiling now. "You're so old," he kids me, "that you'll forget everything soon. I'll have to visit you in the Home. You need to make lists. The Dad to-do list. On your phone." He picks up a pair of brownish gray work gloves. "So?"

"So." I wait. "You were going to tell me what's on your mind."

He puts down the work gloves. He lets out a big teenaged sigh. "Do you want to hear it? You sure?"

"Yes."

"Okay, um, so last month I was, you know, over at Burt and Mom's house." I nod. "And we were having dinner, and I was putting ketchup on, like, my hamburger and stuff, and Burt's going on about some girl he saw walking by that afternoon on the sidewalk, how cute and sexy she was, like it should be illegal for girls to look like that, saying this in front of Mom while he's chewing his food, and then he starts in on me, with the *so-how-come-you-don't-date-girls* thing, and I tell him that I'm only, like, fifteen."

"Uh-huh."

"And he says, looking at me, Well, buddy boy, *I* was already getting pussy when I was fifteen. He says this while we're, you know, at the table, *eating food*. Mom is staring off into space like she's not there except physically. It's just the three of us sitting at the table. Where Pete and Lena were, I don't know. Hooking up as usual. So I take another hit of my hamburger and get up my courage and tell Burt that I'm gay."

"He hadn't figured that out?"

"No. At least I guess not. I mean, who knows what that guy knows? Or Mom, either? He's in this, like, dense fog most days, you ask me. He looks at me like I'm from Yemen or somewhere, and he says, 'You're a fag?' and I say, 'Yup.' Meanwhile, Mom is still trying to figure out where to look, or maybe, I dunno, what to say, and I'm thinking, *Help me out.* Finally she's half-smiling at Burt. I figured she had, you know, told him by now. It's not a big secret, right? Except from him. I mean, he and I don't talk about stuff like that. Or about anything. Finally she says to him, 'I thought you knew,' and Burt shakes his head."

"Let me get this straight," I say. "Burt called you a fag?"

"Yeah," he says. "And then Mom says, in that Mom-voice she sometimes has, 'I love you, Joe, you *know* that, even though you're queer.'"

"Your mom said that?"

"Those exact words."

My heart sinks down into the polar regions.

Joe's been examining the floor of Famous Discount until now, and then he lifts his gaze to me. "It was when Mom said that, I thought: *I kinda want to die, at least a little. I'd be better off slightly dead. Like a coma? A coma would be about right. You'd be there and not-there. I'm too much trouble to everybody, my being queer.* So: those notes I wrote. I mean, you know, if I had a choice, I guess I'd choose not to be gay, but you know, whatever."

I'm trying to think, actually with my head spinning, and that's when I think of what George B. Graham III advised me to do, so I ask Joe, "What do you want?"

In this are-you-kidding voice, he repeats, "*What do I want?*"

"Yeah," I say. "That's what I asked."

"You've never asked me that. Nobody's ever asked me that. Well, maybe when I was five, and you took me to the Santa at the mall, and I wanted a doll, and you got embarrassed."

"Well, I'm asking you now."

"Me? Sometimes I wish I was dead, like I just said? I wish I was happy, occasionally. Sometimes I want to be with Donny." Donny is a school friend of Joe's. They're a little in love with each other, a teenaged boy thing but also more than that. "And sometimes I wish Mom would dump Burt, or kill him, but I guess that'd be messy. Anyway, homicide sucks, right? Because it's, like, a crime?"

And that's when I say, aided by the Generomics blood test, "You don't have to kill that son of a bitch, because I'm going to." It just comes blurting out of my mouth. "With my bare hands I'll do it."

"Jeez, Dad, calm down. No, really, Dad," Joe says, a little anxious now. "You don't have to say *that*." He actually looks smilingly nervous that I'm about to become a murderer. "Holy shit. I mean, whoa, pardner," he says. "It's nice that you're in my corner, but wow. Shouldn't you be getting all parental and, like, telling me to take the long view, perspective-wise?" Someone passes by us on the aisle, maybe eavesdropping on this conversation. "Besides, you try anything on that guy, he'll break you in two, and, duh, murder is against your religion."

"I'm smarter than he is. I'm subtle. Any jury would acquit me in two minutes."

"Dad?" he says. "Can we please end this conversation? Cuz it's not that big of a deal. I mean, my being gay is sorta a game changer, but only for me, and besides, nobody cares about that stuff even in school anymore. There are plenty of queer kids around. Times have changed." Finally he puts down the work gloves. "Don't worry. I won't march in any parades. I won't wear glitter. Anyhow it doesn't matter. It only matters to morons like Burt." Then he says, "I still can't figure out what Mom sees in him." And then, defeated, he says, "I guess he's handsome. Like that even matters, in a person?"

Everybody in our household, including Lena and Pete, knows about Joe's being gay (or his belief that he's gay, which is not quite the same thing), but I haven't mentioned it here until now because it wasn't germane. Besides, he's fifteen, and when you're fifteen, a lot of the cards that fate is going to put in your hand are still being dealt. Some of the cards you're holding are hard to read. The cards are telling you your fortune, a blueprint of the future, but the report is written in a dead language. The lighting is intermittent when you're fifteen, more like lightning than a lightbulb, and you can't see much of anything in the present, much less in the future, and your body isn't helping out. Your body is not your friend when you're that age. If you're a boy, you get erections for no reason at all, pointless hard-ons meant to confuse and confound. If you're a girl, there's the double feature of periods and breasts. No one is safe at that age.

Such were my thoughts as Joe and I entered the house, where Lena and Peter were on the sofa, and Trey was in the recliner chair, and they were all watching the climax of *His Holiness Pope Robot,* where, judging from the excerpt I saw, the robot was being crucified, up there on the cross, bits and pieces of him/it becoming detached, with gyroscopes, wires, screws, circuit boards, and other hardware falling to the ground, and sparks coming out of the robot's head. The poor robot! That's one machine that'll think twice before trying to save humanity again.

Joe surveys the scene before going up to his room. Trey gets up and gives me a quick kiss, while Pete and Lena, their thighs touching, keep watching the robot disintegrate until he's just a mound of spare parts on the ground, only the robot's hands and arms still nailed to the cross. Trey and Lena are having a conversation of sorts about the robot, which I apparently interrupted. Trey's lavender perfume comes to me as a sweet olfactory gift after she has kissed me, sheer profit hanging in the air. "We were just talking," she says, "about how the robot will be resurrected. I think another robot will do it. How's Joe? Did you talk to him?"

"Yes."

"And?"

"Later. Not now."

"Okay."

As we watch, the robot gets miraculously reassembled, as all the parts that came out of it/him fly up back inside him thanks to special effects, and he lights up like a Christmas tree before magically pulling the nails out of his "hands," or else—I wasn't paying close attention—the nails come out of the wood by themselves as if directed by God (possibly a robot Himself?), and the intact robot lowers himself to the ground, stepping gingerly away from the cross. The redeemer business is a hard row to hoe, is the point. If this were an American film, he'd take revenge on everybody, lay waste to a city or two, death rays and hellzapoppin', but this particular robot is without sin and certainly without the customary instincts for revenge, a European robot with a solid memory of historical calamity.

In its Old World way, the robot walks deliberately into the downtown area of some aging European city like Prague, and in a manufactured syntho-voice gives a little lecture about kindness and forgiveness, and then, to no one's surprise, Pope Robot lifts up, rises, *ascends,* into the sky, and a floral "the end" appears on the screen, and Trey announces that dinnertime has arrived—meatloaf again tonight.

Absurd, ridiculous: I have to wipe the tears from my eyes. I've been under a strain.

10

MY EX-WIFE, CHERYL, JOE AND LENA'S MOM (IN CASE YOU FORGOT), first caught my attention in high school because of a scarf she knitted for me, because of her piano playing, and because of a visible bruise she got on her arm from her then-boyfriend hitting her. I saw the bruise when she was playing basketball as the power forward on the girls' team. She was pretty in an unconventional way, with her light brown hair pulled back in a ponytail and schlumpy sweatshirts that put her into a kind of unsexy camouflage disguise, characteristic of some high schoolers who'd rather not be looked at or are black-and-blue somewhere. At that age, self-consciousness can be a problem for anybody; it was for me (I had acne, a slouch, and a bad attitude). She wore the same blue jeans to school day after day, not because her parents were poor but because she didn't want to make any decisions about clothes and because the food stains and other stains on the jeans looked like colorful do-it-yourself action painting.

Actually, her parents *were* poor, now that I think about it. She lived in one of those houses with old broken refrigerators dumped in the backyard and not carted away. A front porch door hung askew on its hinges. But boys saw through her various poverty disguises because she was so pretty—she looked like Jamie Lee Curtis, that sort of haphazard tomboy beauty—and I caught her attention in art class. I couldn't trade on my looks like some guys, so I played the artist card. In those days I had read a lot of Jack Kerouac and other science fiction, and I was drawing and painting on-the-road landscapes, complete with cryptic billboards, *on other planets*. No one else had ever thought of doing this. Originality was on my side. A still life on Mars! Piles of reddish stones! Martians on motorcycles! The extraterritoriality caught her attention. Like me, she wanted to live in another galaxy where things were different from the ground up and freaks were in charge. I gave her one of my paintings, titled *Stratonamia,* the name of the planet I had invented: in Stratonamia, people floated around, and life was happy all the time. Way in the distance, I painted a couple having sex. I was good at small detailing, ultra-tiny brushstrokes or thin lines with number four pencils. You'd miss it if you weren't looking hard. Even our art teacher, Bernie Dayton, didn't notice my tiny people way back there.

How'd Cheryl ever learn to play the piano? Her gift was never explained to me, a complete ongoing mystery. Her parents were too poor to buy a piano but they found one at a flea market. And yet she could play anything she had heard: another of nature's unintelligible accidents. For that matter, where'd she learn to knit? I was one of two boys in our high school who wore a scarf, thanks to her.

She was on the rebound—we were seniors—from yet another jock she was attracted to who had slugged her on the arm and elsewhere. She was attracted to guys like that, violent muscled creeps, and that's who she's with now. She and I were married for a few years—evidence: two children—as she tried out loving a nice guy (me) until she drifted away and hooked up with Burt the handyman, a not-so-nice antisocial hulk. She once complained that I never took her dancing, but that's hardly an explanation for her departure from my life. I'm leaving out a lot of specifics here to save time. You don't want to get specific when your wife, the woman you love, drifts away from you and starts having an affair. She packs a suitcase and is out the door, and you are left there to reassemble your dignity and self-esteem.

My point is, you can't expect sympathy for Joe from the likes of Burt and even Cheryl, who collaborates with him, the muscle-bound oaf. Sympathy was more my job, and Trey's. She's the opposite of a wicked stepmother (a technicality, because we're not married and possibly won't be unless I propose). Also, there's Lena and Pete, who are naturally sympathetic with Joe because they're having so much sex all the time that they think everybody else should have sex all the time—straight, gay, or whatever. I can't wait until the inevitable boredom sets in, to see how they handle it. My daughter and her sleepwalker boyfriend love each other so much, however, they'll probably handle it very well. That's what I like to think.

TREY HAS PREPARED A MEAL FOR ME IN THE KITCHEN. EVERYBODY ELSE has had dinner. Whenever my family gets together, they're always putting things into their mouths. Tonight it's not much of a meal, the usual, meatloaf, but it's micro-love, and all those micro-love deeds add up. Anyway, she sits down with me while I'm eating, after I've said a silent prayer of grace and thankfulness. We start by talking about the robot movie, and I tell her about meeting a crazy person, George B. Graham III, in the town square, and at last we arrive at Joe, Cheryl, and Burt.

"Did you talk to him?" Trey asks, meaning Joe, meaning the suicide notes.

"Yeah. We had a heart-to-heart at the back of Famous Discount."

"I hope you didn't buy any more movies."

"Not this time."

"And?"

"And what?"

"The heart-to-heart," she prompts.

"Well, Burt has been calling him a fag, and Cheryl called him a queer, even though she says she loves him, and they're making him feel like an outcast."

"I thought so. I thought that was happening. I just *knew* it."

I finish my dinner and take Trey's hand. "I guess I have to go over there," I tell her.

She's squeezing my hand and concentrating so hard on me that her forehead creases are growing visible. "I guess you do." She waits. "It's not the sort of encounter you can do on email. So what are you planning on saying to them?"

"I don't know yet. No, wait: yes, I've got it. I'm going to tell them to stop talking to him like that and to apologize."

"Good luck with that," she tells me. "I wouldn't give you good odds."

DAYS LATER, IT'S SATURDAY, THOUGH MY KIDS ARE NOT VISITING THEIR mother this morning, having other things to occupy them, and I'm outside Burt and Cheryl's house, and I'm trying to get inside because of the rain falling on me, beginning to soak my clothes and my running shoes, and because crows are cawing not distantly but close up, jeering overhead, as they watch me get wet, and they're enjoying the sight. Crows are merry pranksters and have opinions. Life is a nonstop party for those birds. I ring the bell, but, knowing Burt and Cheryl as I do, I believe the bell is nonfunctional, like much else in this house. Along with the rain that's falling spitefully, and the crows, laughing at me, the autumnal air is thick and saturated with the smell of forest animals and, distantly, beyond that, the rich human smell of garbage and leaves moldering in the dented gutters. The crows are having a good jest at my expense. I ring the silent bell once more. It's like a dream where you try to get into a house inhabited by malevolent wizards. Then I knock. I am not unexpected: I arranged with Cheryl to come over here last week, suggesting that I might be bringing the money she asked for. In fact I brought it: hundreds of dollars in cash, folded up in my pocket. People usually need incentives to let you in the door. The money is an old-time love offering, thick with nostalgia, in tribute to Cheryl.

And now here's Burt greeting me wearing his usual T-shirt, with a rock band's logo on it, loose pajama bottoms, and he's giving me a provisional smile. "Hey, buddy," he says in a not unfriendly way. I know him: he thinks I've brought him money. The prospect of money makes him hospitable. "Get out of the rain. You're soaked." He comes wrapped in an odor of cigarettes and drugstore cologne. "Come on in." I can tell—anyone could tell—that he and my ex-wife had sex an hour or two ago.

I've been in this house before, of course. The living room is as neat as a pin—coffee table, empty ashtray, and a creased wall poster of the Swiss Alps close to a framed cross-stitch of a blue jay—but that's it as far as appearances go. On a bookshelf are the hardbound collected works of R. Stan Drabble and a paperback, *Masters of Deceit* by J. Edgar Hoover. Hoover's book is an exposé of Communism. In the dining room, the table has an array of unpaid bills—Cheryl has told me that they got an extension on their income taxes, and these papers are, as she informed me over the phone, "tax documents," although they look like ordinary bar receipts to me—and intermixed with the documents are two half-empty beer bottles, with cigarette butts floating in one of them. Two dead flies enliven a place mat. The dining room window has a crack in it, and over there, on that (sort of) sideboard, is a plant, an African violet, dying a prolonged agonizing death. In the kitchen the TV is on. It's a show about duck hunting. This is a house where hygiene is a casual matter. "So I've heard you've gone rogue," Burt says, heading into the kitchen as I take off my soaked shoes.

"Where's Cheryl?" I ask.

"The ball and chain? Upstairs. Doing one of her *projects*." He stops in the doorway. "I don't always know what she's up to. I don't *spy* on her like some people do."

"I never spied on Cheryl. In fact she used to say that I didn't pay enough attention to her."

"Is that a fact," he says. "Want a beer?"

"It's a little early for me," I tell him, glancing at my watch in a threatrical manner. "I never drink beer before lunchtime. What do you mean about going rogue?"

"Oh, you know, that blood test. People around town, the *well-off* people like yourself, have been getting it. It's like a crystal ball for the silk stocking crowd. Secret passageway to the future and all that." He takes a beer out of the refrigerator and twists the cap off. While he's attending to the beer, I take a brief survey of the kitchen. Over there, by the open door leading to the basement stairs, is a waste bin surrounded on the floor by orange peels and banana peels that Burt has thrown in the direction of the bin, and missed. Like many other men, he plays basketball with the food landing or not landing in the trash receptacles. On the kitchen counter is a saltshaker on its side, the spilled salt making a tiny hillock—bad luck—and close by is an opened jar of strawberry preserves alongside two undiscarded sandwich crusts and a strawberry-encrusted butter knife left out unwashed. Water is dripping from the faucet, *plink plink,* a sad and neglectful sound, and I can hardly hear my own thoughts because of the TV, which is showing an old movie, a Western, with some cowboy on horseback who is shooting at Who-Knows-What, and of course the victim turns out to be an Indigenous warrior. There's a general air of confusion, absentmindedness, and incompetence in this kitchen, with Burt as the handsome ambassador of disarray, spreading the kind of domestic chaos associated with the housekeeping of drug addicts who can't be bothered to wash themselves or to pay attention to creeping misrule. Paying attention? Too much trouble! But Burt and Cheryl aren't druggies, that I know of, unless you count beer as a drug. They're just criminally lazy. The world owes them a living, they feel, taking the side of the grasshopper versus the ant. Paying for a new roof is the least of their problems. Any organized activity is a stretch for these two. Apparently the self-help of R/Q Dynamics has not helped *them*. I hate it that my kids have to view this chaos on weekends. At least Burt has not been previously married. At least he has not fathered children of his own. You wouldn't want Burt for a father. In a father contest he would not get a single vote.

"So," Burt says, "word is, I hear that you're embarking on a lawbreaking spree." He takes a swig of the beer. He's so musclebound that he can hardly get the bottle to his mouth. "Inspired by that blood test they say you took."

"Where'd you hear that?" I ask.

"News gets around Kingsboro."

"Yeah, well." The brushfire of rage that's been smoldering inside me gets stoked up a little. "Speaking of crime: story *I* heard was that you fell off a roof. You still hurt? Ribs okay? No brain damage?"

"Naw. I got over that pretty quick." He doesn't like it that I've brought up the rooftop tumble. "I recover fast. I'm as tough as a tank. Smashed the dial of my watch, though. It's not a crime to fall off a roof, by the way."

"Reason I mention it is that Cheryl asked me for a loan. For the roof. She wants a professional."

"Yeah, I know she did. That's how come you're here, right?"

"Business is slow in the handyman department?"

"You always call me a handyman. Where'd you get that idea from? That's not me or what I do. I'm a carpenter, for chrissake. I do subcontracting. I do construction. I'm in the *union*. Which is more than you can say. Anyhow, you haven't answered my question." He takes a swig of his morning beer, and I can tell that he's displeased by my refusal to join him in a moment of jolly male camaraderie enabled by Budweiser. I can see it on his preposterously shining, rancid face: he thinks I'm a prig. My irritation grows like a plant yearning toward the sun.

"What question was that?"

"Your current criminal history. Your profile as a wrongdoer."

"Where'd you hear about this?"

"Word gets around, like I say."

"*As* I say," I correct him. "'Like' is a preposition."

"Goddamn it," he says, loudly, "and fuck you, Brock. You've been doing that since junior high, grade school maybe, correcting people's grammar and stuff, their *shirt color*, you fucking nasty little creep. You used to complain about people chewing with their mouths open. I'm amazed that you're still in business, with your customers or whatever they are, coming in and buying insurance from you, before you get busy and deny their claims, and you sit there telling them to fix their pronouns or whatever the fuck it is they got wrong today, like their hair is, I don't know, parted in the wrong place or they got their shoes on backwards. You drove Cheryl nuts with that stuff," he says, twisting the knife, "criticizing her hairstyle and the color of her lipstick and like that."

I notice that when he gets angry, he steps back, as if he's getting ready to move forward, to pounce, to engage me in a wrestler's headlock.

"I didn't do that. I don't do that," I tell him calmly. "That's not me at all," I say, with a careful voice.

" 'That's not me at all,' " he mocks me, before he pours more beer down his throat. I thought bodybuilders didn't drink beer, but what do I know about bodybuilders except their grotesque faux-superhero cartoon bodies and their narcissism? "So what *is* you? A shoplifter? A guy who runs through red lights? Assaulting little old ladies? Purse snatching? Carjacking? What's your deal?"

"Where'd you hear about this crime thing?" I hate to keep asking, but I have to know.

"Word gets around, *like* I say."

"Word from whom?" I ask him.

"Your faggot son, Joe, that's who. Told me all about your adventures in Famous Discount, shoplifting garden implements and shoe polish and the like. Next I bet I'll hear about you riding a lawn mower out of the garden department into the street. Better watch out you don't get run over."

"What'd you just call Joe?"

"I called him a faggot because that's what he is, currently. Maybe he'll grow out of it. *Maybe.* I'm trying to toughen him up. He needs it. Make a man out of him. *You* won't do it. A man has gotta be a man in this society or else people will walk all over him the way they walk all over you. I ain't prejudiced about faggots as long as they stand up straight and act like men. Besides, nobody likes a doormat except shoes."

I'm advancing toward him. I wouldn't mind getting into a fight with this lowlife even if it means that I get plastered. It would be a joy to hit him. I wouldn't mind killing him, to be honest. But I'd rather see him suffer.

"I guess this means that you don't want all the money I brought over for the roof," I say, with a murderously calm smile on my face. I reach into my pocket and pull out a thick wad of cash.

"We don't need your fucking money," he says, backing up again.

"Actually, we *do* need it," Cheryl says, from the doorway to the living room. Well, there she is, my ex-wife, wearing a housecoat with a flower-pattern fabric. Her radar must be in full rotation, even from the bedroom. She's come downstairs and is watching us. She looks beautiful this morning, Cheryl does, her hair done up with a few streaks of gray in it. How I used to love her! Someone that beautiful, and once upon a time, she picked me! After I invited her to the prom. We experienced several days of true love. Days! That's not nothing. All at once I am disheartened. Burt stops in his backwards progress and glances over at her. She's frowning.

"We talked about this," he reminds her, suddenly and eerily calm.

"Yes, but we need the money, sweetheart," she says, and Burt's face begins, beneath the phony calm, to flame red. For a split second, I think that the "sweetheart" is directed to me, and it takes another moment for me to realize that it isn't, that it's meant for him.

"Drabble talks about people like you," he announces, glaring at me like a bad actor in high school overplaying his part. Okay, here comes the R/Q Dynamics bullshit. When Burt gets mad, it's like getting a stink eye from the homecoming king: a facial expression that's faintly hilarious because it's always accompanied by an R/Q Dynamics sidebar. He puts his beer bottle down carefully on the soiled and unkempt kitchen counter next to an open peanut butter jar, the better to pontificate and edify. "Drabble says that second-rate humans stay at the lower level by not improving themselves enough to stand up for themselves or their rights. He calls them 'ground-floor humans.' They just live on the ground floor of life, is what it is. They're going nowhere. That's you. That's where you are. He says ground-floor and second-level humans are never happily married because the G-force, which all humans have, doesn't flow out of them. It's blocked by your typical shitheadedness. And you are totally basement level. Like a worm. Or a crawling insect. People like you can't rise from the G-force to the H-force, which is where success is located, and also self-ful . . . ful . . . fulfillment." Burt stammers a little when he gets angry. He always has. "You're a small human being, and your son is a pansy. You will never be a falcon."

"Ah," I say, advancing on him. The fighting spirit is completely kindled in me by now. The brushfire is starting to burn the entire forest. I *am* a falcon. He just doesn't realize it. I am thinking of Joe's halfhearted suicide notes and the misery induced by this evil clown in front of me. He's got a size advantage, but he's dumb, and I have the mad fire of bedeviled rage. I would love to punch him. With the money in my fist, I start to poke him on the chest where the logo for the band Sex Miracles is located. The logo is the male upward-pointing arrow enveloped by the sun. Oddly enough, when I start the poking, he backs up more, heading in the direction of the back door and the entryway toward the basement and the garbage and trash containers.

At that moment it dawns on me that he is approaching, unawares, a banana peel on the floor.

"Yeah," he says. "I know all about you. I know you inside out."

"You don't know me. You know nothing."

"Don't make me hit you," he says, taking one more backwards step, and Cheryl lets out a little stifled scream, and then it happens: his right foot comes down on the banana peel, and he falls rearward into the doorway leading down to the basement. He does a little dance at the top of the stairs, trying to get his balance, his arms flailing up and sideways, and then he's falling down the stairs backwards, trying to stop by grabbing at the handrail, but muscle-bound guys are not adept at rapid action, and he's descending too fast to get a grip as he looks at me for an instant, and I think of that guy in Hitchcock's *Psycho* falling in reverse down the stairs after being stabbed by Mother, with an expression two degrees beyond surprise on his face, and that's how Burt is advancing headlong in reverse direction downward until he reaches the bottom, and his head strikes the concrete floor like a bowling ball dropped out of an airplane, and that's it for Burt, poor guy.

Really, all I wanted from him was an apology and some compassion for Joe, not a skull fracture. I didn't ask for that.

11

I DON'T KNOW HOW MUCH YOU MAY HAVE HEARD ABOUT SKULL FRAC-
tures, but the one that Burt got came complete with internal
bleeding. We called 911, and the EMS guys loaded Burt onto a
gurney and then carried him up the stairs. They put him into
a head brace before they did that. Burt was unconscious, more
unconscious than usual, and because of his bulk, the transport
operation of this particular bodybuilder required heavy lifting and
delicate maneuvering up the incline to the kitchen. After all his
talk about my being a basement personality, the basement was
exactly where he himself ended up out cold before they took him
away. Off he went accompanied by the ambulance siren's hee-haw,
followed by Cheryl and me in my car to the ER. I was concerned
about him but ambivalent.

And even if you don't know very much about skull fractures,
you probably know that hospitals have been crowded these days
with virus victims, coughing, hacking, and spitting their way into
ERs and taxing the depleted medical staff. Did I mention that Burt
was and is unvaccinated? You could have guessed it. No immunity
for that guy! But you probably wouldn't have guessed that because
of his fall, he was suffering from a brain hemorrhage, a subarach-
noid hemorrhage, to be specific, as they (later) discovered from
the CT scans, in which blood leaks into the spinal fluid, requir-
ing, I have been told, emergency surgery by specialists who, as it

happens, were not around or available on this particular Saturday. Kingsboro has one doctor who can do that kind of surgery, and he was in Vegas, semiretired, doing whatever they do there. Besides, the ER was crowded with sick people and one person who looked unconscious from a dose of fentanyl, on top of the usual crowd of people who had fallen from ladders or had accidentally stepped barefoot on lightbulbs or slipped in the shower or had a dose of the latest designer disease. Few smiles and very little lively laughter can be seen or heard in the ER, as a rule. Instead, we were confronted with a traffic jam of the sick and disabled and injured and an air of tightly controlled medical hysteria. All the chickens had come home to roost in that place. Chickens everywhere groaning in pain, or sitting there silent thanks to their brand-new suffering.

You notice the prominent clock in the ER, despite the timelessness of the suffering going on nearby.

After a decent interval, I left Cheryl at the ER next to Burt on his gurney. She was crying about Burt and the banana peel that she had disregarded on the floor, and she was careful to say that she didn't blame me for anything that had happened. It wasn't as if I had poked Burt into falling. I was blameless. Wasn't I? She thought so. I wasn't so sure. Had I prayed for his injury? Sometimes you want something and it happens. In the meantime I had given her the big wad of cash for the roof—although, as I was driving home, I could imagine many more payments would probably follow in addition to the tidy alimony I was already paying her. Somehow I intuited that Burt would not be a wage earner anytime soon or ever.

The unconscious mind is a real scamp. And it never takes a vacation. When you wish for something that you don't speak aloud or mention to anybody, the unconscious goes to work to make it come about but goes about the business in sly subterranean ways, using its own invisible tools. Possibilities turn into probabilities and wind up as inevitabilities. I had wanted Burt to suffer. Now he was suffering. He was being punished and was comatose. But it was the wrong kind of punishment, outsized, as if God, or fate, or my own wily unconscious hadn't been paying close attention to what I had asked for, what I had really wanted. Somehow God had lost a sense of scale. Or maybe I had.

I wanted a priest to confess to, but unfortunately I'm not a Catholic, although I did learn grammar from those characters. All I have is you, dear reader.

THE FOLLOWING MONDAY, BURT IS STILL IN THE HOSPITAL'S ICU, AND I'm in my office, sorting through some claims, when I receive a phone call.

"Is this Mr. Hoberson?" the voice, a woman's voice (I think), asks.

"Yes. But it's Hobson."

"Mr. *Brock* Hoberson?"

"Yes."

"Well, I'm calling from Generomics in Cambridge, Massachusetts. I hope you are having a good morning. And a nice day. This is a follow-up call. What we're following up is you. We have been apprised that you have started to fulfill our predictions." A fairly lengthy silence intervened. "Mr. Hoberson? Hello?"

"Hobson. Yes?"

"I was just wondering if you were still there. You yourself may be wondering what I am referring to. I am referring to the theft of some garden shears, yes? From your local Famous Discount in Kingsboro, Ohio? And, a few days ago, a violent assault on the boyfriend of your ex-wife? Do I have this right?"

"Yes. No," I said. "There was no violent assault."

"Burtram Kindlov is, however, in the hospital, is he not? Intensive care? A skull fracture, a subdural hematoma? Is he not in a coma just now?"

"He is indeed."

"And you had an altercation with him this past Saturday morning? During which Mr. Kindlov fell down a flight of stairs?"

"It was an accident," I tell her. "He slipped on a banana peel. Wait a minute, wait a minute," I say. "What makes you think any of these things have happened? How do you know any of this?"

"You have a phone, do you not? With an app that locates your whereabouts?"

"I have an iPhone, yes. But I—"

The woman sighs, as if explaining obvious facts to a dolt. "Mr. Hoberson, we know where you are. Our location supplier, Omniview, knows where you are. The Mowgli app knows where you are and what you buy, et cetera. Anyone who wants to know where and what you are can *easily* target you on your, well, call it your personal landscape, your whereabouts. You're not difficult to follow. You're one of the *easy* ones. Your bulb doesn't burn too brightly with volatility. You're a low-wattage sort of person, a ten-watt character. You walk in your own footsteps. Thus you are easy to reach. We know you're in your office right now. We know about the food stain on your necktie. We know your proclivities. We've been following you, especially now that you're . . . interesting. Following you is like following a child's trail in the snow. That's our job. We follow everybody who has signed up with us and some who have not. In your case the job is untroublesome. And now we have a further business proposition and opportunity for you. We would like to make an appointment with you. You have met Dr. Pilensky?"

"Yes." I look down at my necktie. It's stained. "I have never

installed that Mowgli app on my phone. It's a dangerous app."
Mowgli is a "best friend" app that advises you where to go, what
to buy, what TV shows to watch and what podcasts to listen to,
whom to love, what social media you should pay attention to
down to the tweet level, what dreams to have and to strive for, and
what decisions you should make and how you should go about
making them. Their motto is "Everything we do is tailor-made for
YOU, baby. Who loves you? *We* do!"

"No, to be sure, but *we* have installed it. It is there. As for Dr.
Pilensky, he's in the area even as we speak. He's eager to have a . . .
well, let's call it a conversation."

"I don't want to see him. I don't want to talk to him. Why
should I meet with him?"

"Here there is no why."

"What the hell does that mean?"

"It means that we already know some of the actions that you
are about to take, and we feel it best if Dr. Pilensky advises you
on a plan to protect yourself from, well, call them lawsuits and
prosecution and incarceration and lethal injection."

"A plan? Are you selling something?"

"That would be one way to put it. Another way to put it is to
assert that, given the conditions and the predictable outcomes,
you should buy some insurance from us. For lawyers, and medical
expenses. In this country, medical expenses are the bottomless pit,
the crevasse in the glacier into which the unwary fall. You, of all
people, an insurance agent, should be aware of the necessity to
be insured from the damages that your near-term behavior will,
in all likelihood, incur. The volatility wattage is about to go up.
Soon you will be the rogue of the story."

"What did you say your name was?" I ask.

"I didn't say," the woman says, though I am no longer sure

that the voice is that of a woman, given its interchangeable tenor-alto range. It could be a man. For all I know, the voice could be computer-generated, and I am deep inside a Turing test as I try to guess whether I'm talking to a person or to an AI chatbot machine.

"Care to tell me who you are? And is English your first language? It doesn't sound like it."

"My name is Andrej Cooper. And, yes, English is my first language. I am an American born and raised, originally a Hoosier, I like Boilermaker football and figure skating, I eat occasionally at Burger King with a preference for the double Whopper with cheese, and there are plenty of us here at Generomics who, simple people like you and I, have been born and raised here in the American heartland and who carry around with us good solid heartland American values."

"Not 'like you and I,'" I correct him. "You mean, 'like you and me.'"

I am greeted by a long silence from his/her/their end of the line.

"We see more violence in your future," the voice tells me after that lengthy pause. "Mayhem. And fewer grammatical corrections."

"What are those heartland American values you just referred to?" I ask. "Can you be more specific?"

"We see a murder. Committed by you. We see some fatality, which would not qualify as a heartland value. When would you like to make an appointment with Dr. Pilensky? He will be at the clinic tomorrow. He has an open slot at two p.m. He might be a good person to confer with."

"Fuck you. I'm not a murderer."

"Tut-tut, Mr. Hoberson. Your guilt remains to be seen and *recognized.*"

"It's Hobson. Oh, all right." I sigh, checking my scheduler, which is, unfortunately, clear for most of the afternoon. "But you should say 'with whom to confer.'"

"I see your point, and I will amend my speech. No more terminal prepositions. That's a yes?"

"That's a yes," I say. "Two o'clock."

THAT NIGHT, BEFORE MY CONFRONTATION WITH DR. ("YOU CAN CALL me Al") Pilensky, I hear a clanking from the basement, and when I go down there, I find Joe in a sweatsuit lying on a weight bench, doing bench presses with a set of barbells that I didn't know we had. How did all this equipment get here? Off to the side is a set of dumbbells and a pile of assorted weights. They're arranged on the carpeting in the rec room on the other side of the furnace room. The carpeting is the same orange shag carpeting that was in there when we bought this house seventeen years ago. We keep meaning to replace it, but what goes into the basement has a tendency to stay down there. On the wall we have tacked old yellowing Pan Am travel posters of that dome in Florence (never been there) and Venice—gondolas, etc.—and an old semi-nonfunctional color TV is off to the side near some bookshelves and a pachinko machine that I bought at a rummage sale. It makes a terrible racket when you put the balls in play. Also on the wall is a framed cross-stitch piece with nasty red lettering that says, "Shake it but don't break it." I have no idea what that means or where we acquired it, or why it's still hanging there when no one pays any attention to it. Neither Trey nor Cheryl sews, though Cheryl's aunt Gladys, who lived in Spokane and ran a bait-and-tackle shop near the Behrends River, had a taste for it. But I digress.

Joe is sweating hard when I get there. On his iPhone attached to earbuds he's playing some agent-of-chaos music. He's flat on his back on the weight bench with a barbell suspended at arm's length, and I can see his elbows trembling. He's cut his hair, an action that alarms me. I liked his long, wild hair. He's panting, and when he sees me, he carefully places the barbell in the fixed uprights, with my help. I did some weight lifting when I was a teen in the hopes of bulking up and attracting attention, so I am mindful of the appeal of these endeavors and of their ultimate futility. Saint Paul says in First Timothy 4:8 that "bodily exercise is of little use," but I am careful not to quote Scripture to my son or anyone else at this point. Joe doesn't like it when I invoke Biblical authority, nor do most adolescents, who regard the Bible as little better than an etiquette manual, if that.

With the barbell safely set, Joe sits up and examines me with an expression approaching concern. I worry that his workouts will strain his muscles and joints, but you can't worry about everything when teenagers are living in the house with you. When he finally seems to come back to himself, he blinks his eyes twice, wipes the sweat off his forehead with his sleeve, and says, "How's Burt? Any news?"

I tell him that the guy's still in a coma, still in the hospital, and maybe he'll get better but maybe he won't. Joe is still panting a little. I finish up by saying, "I'm praying for him."

"You are? Why?"

I shrug. "Because I'm sorry he fell down those stairs. Plus, he's with your mother, and he's a human being, and even though I really don't like him, he's got a soul like everyone else. God put us on Earth to take care of other people." Which is mostly true, but anyway it's what I'm saying now, despite my previous behavior. It's a good thing to say even if you don't believe it or act in accord with it.

"Then why'd you push him?"

"I didn't push him."

"Okay, okay, you didn't push him. But . . . this is the thing: I mean for chrissake, I know Burt called me a faggot and everything, and I *know* I wrote those suicide notes, sort of, but, I don't know, you *didn't have to go and kill him,* for my sake, just because he was saying mean stuff to me and because those genetics people said that you could."

"They didn't say that I could. They said that I *might.*"

"Same difference."

"No, it's not." But *did* they say that I could, or I might? "Joe, anybody could kill anybody else at any time," I tell him. "We're all capable of bad violence, except maybe people in wheelchairs. They're not. All I did was poke him in the chest, and then he slipped and fell. And by the way, where did all this weight-lifting gear come from?"

"The guy delivered it in this, like, huge truck. Mom ordered it, and it came. They want me to muscle up. Burt wanted that, and Mom. Me too—I want that. I need to get strong. I need *armor.* I wanna be on TikTok, working out and looking real, like, tough. So that someone could hit me and nothing would happen? Hitting me would be like slugging a file cabinet. They brought it over on Friday, when you were, like, at work. This was, like, before you went over there. And so I'm kinda doing these weights, this workout, and you know what? It feels good. I'm stronger already."

"Good."

"You think I should go to the hospital to visit Burt?"

"No."

"How's my mom doing?"

"All right, I guess. You could text her. She's hanging around in the hospital. They're deciding on Burt's surgery. Has she texted you?"

"Once. It was a weird message. She said to watch out for you.

I didn't know what she meant. I guess I could call her or text her or something. She said you've changed. *Have* you changed?"

"That's a good idea," I tell him, "about getting in touch with her. And have I changed? How would I know?"

WHEN I GET BACK UPSTAIRS, I SEE THAT TREY, MY GIRLFRIEND, IS SITting in the kitchen, gazing out the window at a bird feeder where a junco is picking at seeds. She, Trey, is wearing an expression of wounded patience. I would describe the expression on her face as "pensive," despite the festive faded pink blouse she's wearing and the faded silver-colored slacks she has on, a color that almost matches the silver in her hair. Now that I think about it, the clothes are pensive too, not festive. She's the most decent person I've ever known, softhearted, the sort who would never say an unkind word to a dog or cat, much less a fellow human, and nevertheless I have a feeling that I'm in for it, sweet and diplomatic though she may be. The softness makes it harder to bear.

Her kindness often gets the best of her, and she cries easily. Trey was born in Canada, which may account for her mild disposition, her willingness to see all sides of a quarrel, and her interest in women's hockey and curling. Her mother taught ballet and gymnastics, and Trey inherited from her a physical grace that produces pleasure in the onlooker whenever Trey walks by with her perfect posture and regal bearing and the hint of a smile ignited by private thoughts. Her good posture is a defense to protect her soft heart. Just by looking at her, you wouldn't think she's as tender and sweet as she happens to be. The kindness in her goes all the way down, and her regal posture is deceptive. Her work at the Knoblauch County Park with children has produced in her a tendency to speak softly, so that you sometimes have to lean forward to hear her. So in that soft voice, she says to me, "Let's go for a ride."

"Where?" I ask.

"Oh, anywhere," she says. "We need to talk. No, come to think of it, let's go to the county park. I know a place there," she says with a mysterioso hint. She disappears for a moment, and when she comes back, she has her blue jacket on, and on either side the pockets are bulging with whatever is inside them. I don't inquire about what she's bringing along, me being the guilty party and therefore not at liberty to raise topics of conversation. "All right," she says. "I'll drive."

Behind the wheel of her Jeep, she hums along to the radio, which is playing a tune I don't recognize, though the song is obviously titled "Heartbeat." Wasn't that a Buddy Holly song? It wasn't this one; this tune is different. "Childish Gambino," Trey says, answering the question I haven't asked except through telepathy. I *have* heard of this singer Childish Gambino but haven't heard this song before, which concludes as we are entering the gates of the park. We proceed down the main road and then turn off the paved road onto a nearly invisible dirt trail marked with a sign that says, NO ENTRY. PARK OFFICIALS ONLY. But now I'm thinking of the Buddy Holly song of the same title, which is an antique ballad from the 1950s: "Heartbeat, why do you miss / When my baby kisses me?"

Twigs and branches brush against the sides of the Jeep as we inch forward and the motor grunts. There is hardly a road here at all. It's only there if you know it's there: no tire tracks, just some flattened grass. What does she have in mind? You'd have to have a Jeep or a tough vehicle with a hard, tortoise-like shell to go where we're going. This particular semi-road goes through a canopy of trees, creating darkness on all sides, with thick foliage that reaches in to grab us. No one seems to have been here for weeks. The landscape has been ignored and neglected by humans. I like that.

I know better than to ask where we're headed, but it seems to be a fine and private place, one known only to Trey. Sure enough, when the trees clear, the road opens up to an uneven grassy meadow encircled by maples, colored with their autumnal reds and golds. It's like a sacred circle. At the center of the meadow stands a high pole with a wooden birdhouse and a single circular entrance. The birdhouse is in the shape of a miniature garage. A bird I can't identify nervously flies in and then peeks out at us. After saying, "Wait here," Trey gets out of the Jeep. When the bird sees her, it seems to calm down. The bird *knows* her. Somehow I'm not surprised.

After walking to the center of the meadow, a few feet beyond the birdhouse, Trey reaches into her right pocket and pulls out what must be birdseed. She holds it in her palm and stretches her arm out and raises her palm to the sky. A few seconds pass, and the bird I saw earlier notices her and flies down to her hand, picks up a seed or two, and takes off. And after that, this happens: from the other side, the clumped trees to my left, a deer emerges, a doe, full-grown, shivering with fear and anticipation, one more animal that appears to be well acquainted with Trey. The bashful doe nears my girlfriend, one brown-eyed creature to another. Trey reaches into her other pocket. She pulls out some food pellets. Extending her left hand, she holds the pellets while this deer ambles toward her and begins to eat from her palm. Meanwhile, the bird, on a return visit, takes some more seed from Trey's right hand before it alights on her cap.

The deer is munching on the pellets and seems ready to root its muzzle in Trey's jacket pocket when another bird flies down and grabs some seeds, and one more deer emerges from the woods. The Saint Francis spectacle will not stop. Birds and deer: I wouldn't be surprised if a possum, a skunk, and a porcupine, all of them known by their proper names, waddled out for a free lunch. I can't quite breathe as I watch my beloved feeding these animals. She is smiling, she is greeting them. I feel unworthy of her. I love her and I can almost love the dramatization she's giving me, a demonstration or maybe a proof of soul. I once thought you weren't supposed to feed wild animals, but I have just changed my mind on that issue. What I'm saying is that she's offering food to these animals, but, really, she is *caring* for them. *This pastorale* is the one she inhabits. This is her world, her life. Who knows what animals think? But at that moment, I would have bet that they felt comfortable around her. She probably has an aura visible only to them.

Watching her, I feel my chest tightening. She is a gold-standard human being.

When she's finished, she turns around and comes back to the Jeep. The docile animals follow her. One bird settles down on the hood, and the two deer approach the driver's side once she's sitting there.

Trey's first husband, Michael, died young. They hadn't had any children, hadn't gotten around to it yet. As a result, she carries around a sad cheerfulness; she glows with it. The animals sense it. They come to the driver's-side door, begging.

"This is my secret," she says quietly. "Don't tell anyone."

At that moment I think of the way she makes love: at first shyly, like an adolescent, before she becomes greedy and passionate, also like an adolescent. She rarely initiates sex with me, but once she starts, she is avid. Her avidness is part of the animal in her. But she always retains some part of her past, of the man she loved and lived with before she loved me. If I were to marry her, she would still be a widow. Her love for her first husband won't ever die. She believes in loyalty to the dead. Sometimes I can tell that Michael's spirit is still inside her: he may be dead but was not liquidated and is accompanying her somehow.

Eventually the deer wander away. But the bird—it's a nuthatch,

Trey tells me—stays, nervously flitting around in front of our windshield. It's as if the bird is engaged in courtship behavior: it apparently wants Trey to come back out.

"How long have you been feeding these animals?" I ask.

She shrugs. "Why? Does it bother you?"

"No. I was . . ." I don't know how to finish the sentence. I don't have the right adjective.

"You can't imagine," she says. "You can't imagine what it feels like when a wild creature eats from your hand. The birds are as light as feathers. They give off . . . these tremblings. And the deer don't actually like people, so at first they snort at you, scared sounds. But they're hungry, so they come near to me, and now they're used to it, and they don't mind me that much anymore."

"They like you."

"No, they don't," she says. "They only tolerate me. Instinct guides them. Something tells them about humans. They sense our creepiness. So they're wary."

"Honey," I say, "sweetheart, why are we here?"

She's still gazing at the nuthatch that's looking back at her. An exchanged glance between woman and bird. I look down at Trey's thighs and feel a strange onset of desire. "You're changing," Trey says. "Ever since that blood test. You're becoming a different person. A different *man*. Something has descended on you. I don't know why or how it's happening, but it scares me."

"I'm the same guy I always was," I tell her. "Is this because of what happened to Burt?"

"No. Yes. No, you're not the same guy, even if he hadn't fallen down those stairs. I can tell. Even when you're sleeping, you're different. I still love you but I'm worried about you and what you're going to do. I want you back the way you were before you were tempted by those people."

"They didn't tempt me. It was just a blood test."

"You think so? These people have cooked up a bad business to make money in the worst way. Brock, they're evil. They put you on a path. They gave you permission to do anything and everything. Everything is permitted once they say so. Don't you see?"

"That's not who they are," I tell her. "They're just a bunch of scientists and doctors going around making predictions."

"What if they're scammers? Or crackpots with a two-thousand-dollar phony blood test? First they sell you this; then they sell you whatever's next. Who's the crackpot now? How do you know it's not a scam?"

"Well, they're *doctors*. From *Cambridge,* Massachusetts. I'll meet with them tomorrow."

She makes a sound that I have to reproduce here as "Pfffftttt"— a noise of disgust and revulsion. Then she says, "That's what they say. You haven't even looked them up on social media. Everyone else would have. But you, you got taken into their carnival tent right away. It's not only the money they took. It's what they did to you. They're not honest people. They said you could be someone else, someone awful. First you're Jekyll, Mr. Nice Guy, and then you get to be Mr. Hyde. I want the old Brock back." She waits. "I lost one husband. I don't want to lose another."

"He's still here," I tell her. "Me," I add quickly. "*I'm* still here." Then: "Jekyll. The good one."

"I hope that's true. I wish it were true."

Sitting in her Jeep, with two deer walking away, I can't think of anything else to prove myself, to prove I'm me. What can you do to prove you're still yourself to someone who thinks otherwise?

12

AN UPDATE ON BURT'S CONDITION: NO CHANGE. THE COMA PERSISTS. My first victim, and he's in stable but critical condition.

When I get to the clinic the following day, the receptionist tells me that the representative from Generomics will not be meeting me here, but elsewhere, in the Bagley Building, Room 223, four blocks away. I heave a sigh, get back into my car in the light drizzle, which doesn't justify an umbrella but manages to soak me anyway. I had quarreled with the clinic's receptionist, an argument that had also weighed down and dampened my mood.

"They were supposed to be *here*," I told him. "The Generomics people."

"Well, they're not." The receptionist gives me a hostile smile.

"They could have called me."

"Apparently they didn't."

"What reason did they give?" I asked.

"They didn't give one. Maybe the other doctors here didn't want the Generomics project managers around."

"This is very unprofessional."

"Couldn't agree more," the receptionist said, twiddling a pen in midair. "Very unprofessional. But I'm not responsible. I had nothing to do with it. I'm only the messenger."

"Why the Bagley Building?"

"They didn't tell me. Have a nice day!"

Therefore I return to my car and drive the short damp distance to the Bagley Building, designed by that semi-famous local architecture firm, Dunsheath & Associates, known for "simplicity with style," which in this case means brutal fortress concrete and slit-like azure windows that reveal nothing on either side. The Bagley Building has offices for lawyers, tax accountants, dentists, architects, and that ilk. I could have moved my insurance office over to the Bagley Building, but I didn't like the strange hum in the hallways or the gray linoleum or the plastic potted ferns, or the threatening tone of the mechanical voice in the elevators announcing floors. Also, the building smelled of black mold and cancer. The slit windows looked out at a strip mall whose anchor storefront was a payday loan office.

Holding a scrap of paper with the office number I'm supposed to go to, 223, I open the door and find myself in an Orwellian reception room with two chairs, no pictures, no receptionist, no table with reading matter, and only a rectangular area on the wall, darker than its surroundings, where a picture once hung. In the corner is a cage in which someone's pet white rat is sleeping. What's *that* doing here? On the opposite side of the room is an interior door whose built-in window has been covered over with cloth. From the ceiling comes background music, a soupy rendition of "Here Comes the Sun" arranged for strings and alto sax. I wish George Harrison hadn't signed away the rights to that song, so that these studio musicians could make a mockery of his joy. This song was never meant to be background music. It's *foreground* music: bliss and delight are right around the corner, it tells us. They're imminent. But not now, not in this place, they aren't.

After about five minutes, the door to the office's interior opens, and out comes a not unattractive woman carrying a clipboard to which is attached a ballpoint pen. She's tall, my height, brown-haired, officious, and expressionless in that bureaucratic way we're all getting used to. Her fingernails are painted bright red, and she's wearing red pumps and a white smock. Covering her eyes are comically oversized black-framed glasses. They don't fit her and give her an owlish appearance. She pushes them upward onto the bridge of her nose as I study her for clues. After fixing her glasses, she checks off a box on the clipboard and turns to me to ask, "Mr. Hutson?"

Here we go again. You'd think my name wouldn't be a challenge to most sentient adults. "No. Hobson. Brock Hobson." I stand up. "That's the same mistake that Dr. Hasselblad made and then Dr. Pilensky made it, too."

"A computer error. Unusual name," she opines. "I don't believe I've ever met a Hobson before." She writes something down on the clipboard. "I am Dr. Pilensky."

"Are you married to the other Dr. Pilensky? Alan Pilensky? He's the first person from Generomics to whom I talked."

"No," she says. "We're not married. Nor are we siblings. It's just a coincidence."

"That's the strangest thing I ever heard of. If that just doesn't beat everything."

"I can understand your astonishment."

"Do you mind telling me your real name?"

"I'm sorry, but I *would* mind, very much. I can't do that." She waits. "I wish I could but I can't, so I won't." She waits. "Company regulations. For you I don't have a real name. In here, that is, in these offices, I am Alicia Pilensky. Care to come into the consulting room, Mr. Hobson?" She directs toward me the remnant of a smile, which causes cracks to appear in her face. "Please."

"Um, sure. Okay."

She ushers me into a very plain area, the sort of room where nothing of value can possibly happen. The slit window has a view of the parking lot, and next to the window are two diplomas, one for Dr. Barth (Who is he? Is he here?) and Dr. Horner (ditto). When I go to sit down in the center of the room, I discover that the chairs are bolted to the floor. They're made of straight-backed, uncushioned wood, and the chairs are placed so close to each other that you have to sit sideways so as not to knock your legs against the person sitting across from you, in this case "Dr. Pilensky," or whoever she is. Over there in the corner is a lamp made of pinewood, probably from a do-it-yourself discount furniture store whose merchandise you must assemble on your own, following the cartoonish directions to turn the little wrenches and screws they enclose. In the other corner, attached to the wall, is an old faded calendar for the year 1994 showing downtown Amsterdam, and, below that, a mahogany secretary desk on which there are no loose papers and only one book, a novel, Lloyd C. Douglas's *The Robe,* which I read in sixth grade for Sunday school. It's just here for show. No one would voluntarily read that book in the twenty-first century.

"Now then," the so-called Dr. Pilensky says to me, "how're you doing, Mr. Hobson? Everything shipshape?"

"I guess so," I reply, "except for my ex-wife's boyfriend in the ICU. That's not particularly shipshape, that situation. That ship may be sinking. I hope not. By the way, what's the white rat doing out there in the waiting room?"

"I call the rat 'a coming attraction.' The rat's name is Bobby. But we need to talk about something else. I have a readout from our computer, our central mainframe in Cambridge, Mass., and because it signaled an upcoming manifestly critical event enacted by you, we thought that we needed a person-to-person consult with you ASAP."

"Sort of a code red situation, huh?" I turn slightly. This chair is the most uncomfortable one onto which I have ever had to plant myself. My sitting extremities are already beginning to signal the birth and progress of pain, and my sciatica, dormant for the last few days, has yawned and awakened. A little house fire has been ignited in my left leg. Pains like this, those ultra-quiet bodily screams, really wake you up.

"A code red? You could say that. That would be layman talk. Anyway, right here is the now. And what I mean by the 'now' is our new, upgraded computer readout from our mainframe. They fed it brontobytes of information about you. And it's one of those good news, bad news deals," she says, pointing down at the paper on her clipboard.

"Um, okay," I say, trying to get comfortable on my uncomfortable chair. "What's the bad news?"

"You're going to commit a murder."

"You don't say." I try to keep calm. "But I'm not a murderer," I inform her.

"Well, that's not what it says here."

"The computer is mistaken. What's the good news?"

"Ah." She straightens up and offers me a smile. "We have engaged the services of a law firm, Dawes, Walling, Nadler & Trach LLP, and we are offering you an insurance policy so that if you *do* commit the aforementioned murder as predicted by the computer's algorithm, we will cover all legal expenses incurred by your defense as represented by Dawes, Walling. They're based in New York City—very nice offices on the twenty-third floor just south of Grand Central on Park Avenue, I must say—and in Ohio they have regional branches in Cincinnati and Cleveland. They're tough. Real ankle biters. If John Wayne Gacy had engaged the services of Dawes, Walling, he'd be free right now, blowing up balloons as per usual and wearing his polka-dotted Pogo the Clown suit at kiddie birthday parties. Same with Jeff Dahmer. If he had been lawyered up with these white-shoe litigants, he'd be out on the prowl in Milwaukee this very minute, wreaking havoc. Look out, World, am I right?" She took a breath. "And Ted Bundy? Well, you get the picture."

"I don't think I like those comparisons. I don't care for the company you're putting me into."

"Well, I'm joking, of course. Perhaps a mistake of . . . tone? Still, I can't help it if you have no sense of humor," she says. "As I say, this insurance policy would protect you from all legal expenses. We feel that it's a real bargain, and of course you of all people know the value of insurance. Besides, when it comes to a defense for felony murder, you can't be too careful. Here's the sum that would qualify you for the services by Dawes, Walling." She writes out a figure on a sheet of paper on her clipboard and then shows it to me.

"That's a lot of money." I wait. "I'll bet you get a kickback. You know, I sell insurance myself. I'm an agent. It's my profession. I'd have to see the policy. I would need to read the fine print."

"We're quite agreeable to that eventuality," she says, with that same ghost of a smile, the sort of mangled facial expression you get when an unpleasant person tries to be sociable. "Fine print is no problem. You want a magnifying glass? I can send the policy to your email later today. The policy has been written up by the good people at Glickman-Doerr Consolidated Life and Casualty. Let me say right now that I count myself as pleased that you're interested in our offer. Of course we don't expect you to make up your mind right away, but, given the imminent nature of this crime you're about to commit, speed is almost certainly of the essence. And while we're on the subject, in case you're interested, Generomics is prepared to sell you, at below cost, a Finn 23, a real bargain, though of course we're only thinking of your well-being here. That is one excellent defensive firearm." She pauses for breath. "A Finn with a full magazine clip is, how shall I put it, *decisive*. Payment for the Finn can be deferred almost indefinitely.

And anyway, you know what they say about a good defense being a good offense."

"No. What do they say? And can you explain to me why Generomics doesn't have a website?"

"Security. Security pure and simple," she says with a twist of her head, sweeping a bit of hair behind her ear. "We don't want the trouble that people are talking about when they talk about trouble."

"What else are you selling?" I ask.

"Well, we detected, from the blood test, that you will need a companion pet. Do you own a dog?"

"No. Didn't you know that? I thought you knew everything."

"So the answer is 'No'? In that case, Bobby, the white rat you saw in the waiting room, is for sale. The little guy needs a home. I can't say enough in praise of him. People disparage rats, of course, but Bobby is super-companionable. He's clean. He'll eat right out of your hand. He loves to be tickled. Did you know that rats can laugh?"

"No."

"This one can." She takes a moment to chuckle. "It's like a little tiny wheeze."

"Doctor," I say, "I feel that I have become enmeshed here in a very complicated scam, if you don't mind my saying so."

"I do mind. I'm sorry you feel that way," she says. "Oh, before I forget: Generomics is moving into the field of predictive consumer spending and demographics, the genetics of consumerist time and motion. We could be very helpful in your work as an insurance agent, prediction-wise. And *not* incidentally, how were your dreams last night?"

"Fine."

"We have ways of monetizing dreams, if you're interested. These are bargain dreams. We could bring you in on the ground floor, pennies on the dollar. We have a dream for sale to straight men that is guaranteed to bring you to a harmless no-hands orgasm in the safety of your own home. Speaking of which, how's your son, Joe?"

"This is crazy. I'm getting out of here. And Joe is none of your business."

"We understand that he is pumping iron. In two years we believe that he'll look like Lou Ferrigno, that is, if he consumes the right protein shakes and learns to eat red meat. We have designed a diet for him and a program of martial arts. If he follows our curriculum, he'll be positioning himself to kick some hetero ass in no time flat. Beware a gay bodybuilder who's a martial artist! That's just common sense. With our coaching, there'll be no more bullying of *that* kid."

"Why Ferrigno? Why not Schwarzenegger?" By now I am humoring her.

"No. That would be unattainable. But if he plays his cards right, he'll be a teenaged Hulk."

"I'm outta here." I turn, and my left foot knocks against hers. She frowns.

"I feel that I may have overplayed my hand," she says, tilting her head with stagy remorse. "Sometimes I drive to the hoop a little too hard. Are you sure that you don't want to buy the insurance policy whose benefits I have outlined for you in detail today? After all, when a felony murder is on the horizon straight ahead of you, it's wise to prepare yourself and take stock." She removes her oversized glasses so that I can see her brown eyes more clearly. "Brock," she says tenderly, "Mr. *Hobson*. We want only the best for you. I myself want the best for you. I'm concerned for your welfare. For example, the Finn 23, an excellent weapon, I recommend it. I feel—and forgive me if I'm being a little forward—I feel that *we have a connection.* A *strong* connection, based on established mutual need. May I write down your name for this insurance policy? The people at Dawes, Walling are expecting your reply. They'll want to know your answer by four p.m. today so that they can prepare their defense of you. You need to get ahead of the curve on this one. You'll need to protect yourself and your family."

"How much did you say the cost of Bobby is? The rat? Out there in the waiting room?"

"We'll just put it on your account." She touches my forearm. "It's a healthy rat. And fixed. He's out of the procreation game. Plus he's had all his shots. We trust you."

13

AT OHIO STATE, I ONCE TOOK A LECTURE COURSE IN THE HUMANITIES Department, and the subject was—I hope I'm remembering this title correctly—Myths That Rule Our Lives. There was a segment on prophecy and soothsaying. The course was taught by Professor Gmitro, who had been drafted into the war in Vietnam before getting a degree in classics at the University of Illinois, where he studied under the palindromic professor, Revilo P. Oliver. Like many professors Gmitro cultivated a certain eccentricity: on his left wrist were three watches, and his sport coat's plastic pocket protector contained upward of twelve ballpoint pens. Gray hair sprouted in a random uncombed pattern on his head. Often he lectured with an unlit cigarette between his fingers. It was a prop, the same cigarette day after day, a Camel. You couldn't tell whether he was in possession of the ideas he spoke about or whether the ideas were in possession of him—whatever it was, his mind seemed to be perpetually churning, the evidence being the dark half-moons of sleeplessness under his eyes. His hands shook. Overhead, the old fluorescent lights in Anderson Hall all snapped and flickered as they would in a horror movie.

He rarely looked at us, his students; instead, he gazed down at the floor as if the truth were located there among the scuffed-up tiles. He lectured without notes in perfect sentences and paragraphs like a man under a spell, and you'd think all this would bore you, but, no: it was high voltage, as if your behavior and the behavior of humanity through all of history were on the line, and the truth about everything was being revealed at last after being hidden under a rock. He quoted lines in Greek and Latin and German and then offered on-the-spot translations. He talked about Sophocles and Nietzsche in the same breath, the birth and death of tragedy. He walked with a limp, and the rumor went around that he'd once been wounded by a land mine. He didn't appear to live in the world we lived in. He himself was part of the world of myth. Sometimes, quoting poetry in ancient Greek, he would address us directly in the lecture hall, raising his voice almost to a shout, speaking a language that none of us understood, but somehow we did understand the feeling behind it, and for moments at a time, we got it, we were there, at the heart of the heart.

Cassandra, he said, had been a priestess of Apollo, and she lived under a curse: she knew what would happen, having been given a prophetic gift, but no one listened to her or believed her. In one version of the story, she slept with her brother in a temple dedicated to the god Apollo, and the snakes slithered up to her and whispered in her ears. Prophecy, Professor Gmitro told us, in the Christian and Judaic traditions is given to those with a special relationship to God, and the gift of foresight is typically refused. Isaiah and Ezekiel and Jeremiah were burdened with their gift. Predicting the future comes with a deep darkness, he said: Macbeth is ruined by the future that the weird sisters reveal; knowing what the future holds, Professor Gmitro told us, is not a blessing but almost invariably the opposite. Pliny the Elder referred to crystal balls used for clairvoyance and soothsaying, and he warned against them. Astrology, in one of its forms, reveals the future, to no one's benefit.

"In myth," Gmitro told us, "knowing the future is usually a catastrophe for the one who knows. In the ancient world, the psychic, the prophet, the soothsayer are all honored but also cursed and the news of the future is *always* bad news. In these stories the future is never rosy because a rosy future is not newsworthy. The person who carries the bad news is an outcast and often an enemy. The gods may know the future, but we should not meddle with such knowledge. It is against nature to know what will happen before it happens.

"If someone offers to tell you your future," Professor Gmitro advised us, "start walking in the other direction."

I still have the notes I took in that class.

You're going to commit a murder. Those were her exact words to me.

WHEN I GET HOME, CARRYING BOBBY THE RAT, IN HIS CAGE, LENA IS alone in the house, sitting at the kitchen table, reading a biology textbook and absentmindedly eating dry Cheerios from a bowl. Seeing the rat, she perks up immediately, and I'm a little jealous that the sight of the rat makes her happier than the usual sight of me.

"A white rat!" she exclaims happily. "Where'd you get it?" She has always loved animals.

"The Generomics people sold it to me," I tell her. "His name's Bobby. They said I needed a pet."

"Ooooohhh." She opens the rat's cage, and, sure enough, after a moment's hesitation and sniffing, the rat hops out onto Lena's hand. With her other hand she feeds Bobby a single Cheerio. He just gobbles it up and then, still in her hand, sits up, looks at her lovingly with his tiny pink eyes begging for another breakfast token, which she feeds to him. Then she starts to pet his back, and the rat smiles, a little animal suck-up brownnoser. I seem to be watching women feed animals lately, like one of Christ's parables about charity and gentleness in the Gospels. "No kidding, this is the best rat ever," she tells me. "May I have him?"

"I guess so, for now. See what Trey says. She may be phobic about rats. They also gave me a bag of food pellets for him," I tell her, pointing at the bag next to the cage. "We need to do some research on what to feed him."

"Oh, they'll eat anything. Including salad. And you got him and he's here because why?"

"The Generomics people said I needed to stay calm, take care of some living entity like that rat, that's why. Is there any news about Burt? And how's your mom?"

"They moved Burt into a long-term-care facility this morning," she says, feeding Bobby a third Cheerio. "He's still out of it. Mom's going to be talking to you about it. The money, especially. She's worried about the money. She's worried about being totally wiped out. You know, medical bills? Like, catastrophic?"

"Oh, okay. Where's your boyfriend?"

"His name's Pete."

"I know, honey. I know his name. I'm just trying to lighten the mood."

"He's at Photography Club. At school. Or maybe Chess Club. I can't remember which one it is today. What's today?"

"Tuesday."

"Then it's Chess Club. He should be here in a few minutes." She takes out her phone to see if he's texted her, but he hasn't. The rat is now walking up her arm, grabbing hold of her sleeve with its little claws as it makes its way to her shoulder. Once it's perched on her shoulder, it settles down there. "Can he have dinner with us?" She means Pete, not the rat. "I've got the baked potatoes in the oven, the meatloaf is warmed up, and I've got the salad makings ready."

"Sure. Pete can have dinner here. I mean, he usually does, so why not tonight? You don't really need to ask."

"Yeah," she says, smiling. Bobby the rat seems quite contented, resting on Lena's shoulder. It begins to lick its fur to clean itself. "He loves me," she says, referring to Pete, I think. "Daddy, what else did those Generomics people tell you? You do realize you're being scammed, don't you?"

"Yes. I know. They're trying to sell me an insurance policy. Me! I should be selling *them* a policy. They say . . . they say I'm going to murder somebody."

"Wowza. Kinda upping the ante, right?" She takes a Cheerio from the bowl and pops it into her mouth. "Big desperado. That's you, Dad. I guess they've been following your browser history."

"They don't know me. I've been praying for guidance through all this and so far my prayers haven't been answered."

"Who would you murder, anyway?" she asks. "In your world, who's even murderable? Anybody?"

"I don't know. I mostly don't have any enemies," I tell her, being careful not to mention Burt. "Nobody I hate. I'm acquainted with some people I don't like very much, but that doesn't count." Am I being a hypocrite? Sort of, for her sake.

"*Everybody's* got enemies," she says. "You, too. There are a few people at school I wouldn't mind killing. Besides, those scammers have given you a get-out-of-jail-free card, right?"

"Lena, you don't mean that. You wouldn't really kill anybody. Not really." Maybe after all I should sign up for the insurance that would pay for the services of Dawes, Walling, that is, if I ever discover I need to kill somebody. But murder seems to be against my principles. And God's. Murder is a sin, I'm quite sure.

Bobby the rat is growing sleepy. Resting on Lena's shoulder, his eyes heavy, he's apparently about to take a nap. He is indeed a companionable rat.

"I meant what I said," Lena tells me. "I mean, okay. Listen, the biggest thing that's ever happened to me in my life is Pete, the way he loves me. He loves everything about me, Daddy, everything that I do. And *am.* I never thought this could happen. We share wavelengths, him and me. I mean, I know *you* love and care about me, but you're only my dad. With Pete, it's different. When we're together, we're superhuman." She raises her eyelids so that she's almost glaring at me, ready for a challenge. "We're, like, *above* everything, looking down. Everybody envies us, how cool we are, everybody who's not in love. And it's not just teen love, puppy love. It's real. And not just the sex, either, though that's great. I mean, it's true. It's so *beautiful.*

"And there are these girls in school who've seen Pete and I together, and you can tell they want what we've got for themselves, what we *have,* they want that, and because they want him, the way he loves me, they hate *me.* They're so envious."

I can see from her face that she's getting carried away, but I let her continue. This time, I know better than to correct her grammar. "And because they hate me, they flirt with him. He ignores them, of course, doesn't pay any attention to them, but some of them are pretty, this skank Regan especially. She goes to school with her boobs almost hanging out and a pendant, so you *have* to look at her chest. She doesn't give you a choice. She *makes* you look. She tries to be around him, getting in his way. And she stares at Pete, making eyes at him."

"And your point is?"

"Sometimes when I see her doing that," Lena says, *"I just want to kill her.* Just sayin'. Really want to kill. Like, I finally have something in my life that's better than anything else, and she wants to take it away from me. I could actually murder her in real life. Passion, right?" She waits. "Incidentally, where's Trey?" She pulls out her phone to check it for texts. Nothing there.

At that moment Joe comes in from the backyard, where he probably dropped off his bicycle. He's wearing jeans and a tank undershirt, even though with early Ohio winter here, the air's too cold for what he's got on, but I guess he wants to show off the muscles he doesn't have yet but plans to acquire. His hair is shorter in back, but in front still hangs down over his eyebrows like a curtain. When I see him, my heart lifts. He's in his socks. Glancing over at his arrival, Lena says, "Well, if it ain't Mr. America. In person."

Half-ignoring his sister as he usually does, Joe says, "Fuck you, Lena. Hi, Dad. Did you know there's a package for you out on the front stoop? It's real heavy." He gives his sister a bored once-over and then perks up when he sees Bobby. "Hey, where'd that white rat come from?" Instantly he's at his sister's side, and he's stroking the rat, whose eyes stay closed with pleasure like a stray dog that, after many adventures, has finally found a home.

"His name's Bobby," Lena tells him. "Dad gave him to me."

"Where were you?" I ask Joe. Then to Lena: "I don't remember saying that the rat was yours."

"I was out," Joe informs me, without elaborating. He's an expert at information without content. All teenagers do this cloak-and-dagger undercover behavior, maybe the gay kids especially. They don't want you to know the first thing about them. Probably he was over at Donny's house. "Now I'm back."

The front door slams, and in walks Pete, first taking off his shoes in the entryway. As a virtual family member, he's beyond ringing our doorbell. Now he's here in the kitchen, wearing his sweats. He's been running again and is damp. Why doesn't he ever shower before coming over here? I think Lena probably likes the smell of him. "Hi, everybody," he says, as he comes into the kitchen. "So everybody's here? Hey, babe," he says to Lena, giving her a quick peck on her forehead, which causes Bobby to wake up, as Lena feeds him a food pellet. This animal is going to get fat fast in this household. "Where'd this rat come from?" he asks me. "Looks like a real nice rat."

Joe says, "Yeah, it likes to be petted. Dad got it somewhere. Lena says he gave it to her but he didn't really."

"He didn't?" Pete asks. He sidles in and leans against my daughter, who leans back toward him. If this isn't love, I don't know what it is.

"I heard you were at Photography Club," I say to Pete.

"Naw," he says. "I was running." Pete is on the track team. "Photography Club was yesterday." It occurs to me that maybe Pete hasn't been jogging but has been stepping out to see this Regan person whom Lena mentioned, but I don't allow that idea to land; I don't even give that idea any airspace. The best explanation is usually the simplest: he was jogging. "Where'd you say this rat came from?"

"Those Generomics people gave him to me, or they sold it to me. They were a little vague about the cost of the rat."

"They *gave* you a rat?" Joe asks. He's found a protein bar and is eating it. I think: *Look at this kid. I hope someone his own age loves him eventually.* "How come? Are you, like, saying it's, like, a free rat?" He thinks for a minute. "There's no such thing as a free rat. It's like a free lunch. No such thing."

"I don't know. They told me I'd need a companion." I don't mention the imminent murder I'm going to commit, according to them, and the consequent need for a rat pal.

My daughter says, "What about Trey? Isn't she your companion? Your partner? She mostly lives here. She sleeps here and you teach Sunday school with her and she cooks meals and everything. What do you need another companion for? Especially a rat?"

"I know," I say. "Isn't everybody hungry? I should start dinner."

"I already sorta started it already," Lena tells me.

"Um, yeah," Pete says, with his arm around Lena. "I'm starved." You can tell they both want to make love. It never stops with those two. They'll get over it.

At that moment Trey arrives—I heard her Jeep, with its bad muffler, outside, as she parked—and like everybody else here, she takes off her shoes so she's wearing socks, and when she blows into the room, she surveys the scene and says, "Well, if it isn't the entire Addams Family." She's about to kiss me when she sees the rat on Lena's shoulder, and she lets out a little scream, which startles the rat, who climbs down Lena's shirt and takes cover in the shirt's front pocket, and then, like a cartoon character, lifts up its head to peek out. "My God," Trey says. "Who's *that*?"

"It's Bobby," Lena and Joe say almost simultaneously. Then Pete says, "Those Generomic people gave him to Mr. Hobson today. It's a white rat," he tells her, unnecessarily.

"Why?" She smiles. "Why didn't anybody ask *me* about a pet rat?"

"It's complicated," I tell her. "You didn't get the blood test. And it just sort of happened. Lena, maybe you should take Bobby and his cage upstairs while we're making dinner. I don't think it's a good idea to have a rat around when you're tossing a salad or when you're heating the meatloaf or steaming the vegetables. He might get too excited. He might pee on us. He's still a stranger in this house. He has to get used to our routines."

"*What* routines?" Joe asks. "You mean *your* routines? Dad, you want me to go get that package?"

"Oh, yeah," Trey says. "There's a package for you. I saw it out there, and I brought it in and put it on the floor in the entryway. It's quite heavy. It's like a gold ingot from your secret admirer."

Lena and Pete are headed upstairs, Pete carrying the rat's cage, and Lena's holding Pete's other hand. She told me that as soon as they graduate from high school, they're going to get married, and I believe her. They have an unofficial, off-the-books engagement. They've both applied to Ohio Wesleyan, and they'll probably both get in, so they're going to go there together a year from now as young semi-married undergraduates. Who knows if the marriage will last? I wish them luck. But there's no point in getting ahead of ourselves. Joe follows them upstairs to go to his room. Trey slumps a little against the counter before opening the refrigerator to get the makings for salad onto the countertop. But Lena has already taken them out, and the lettuce and green peppers are in a Tupperware container next to the fridge.

"Hard day?" I ask.

She nods. "One of the owls got loose, but it came back. They usually come back, those owls."

"I thought they couldn't fly."

"They can fly. But mostly they don't want to. They're sedentary. They sit and think. They just want to hang out and be owls."

"I see."

"Didn't you talk to those Generomics grifters at the clinic today?"

"They're not at the clinic anymore. They're in the Bagley Building. They *moved*. And, yes, I did talk to them. A Mrs. Dr. Pilensky this time. Don't ask," I say, holding up my hand. "They're all named Pilensky. All of them."

"What'd she say?"

And that's when I tell her about the offer of an insurance policy to pay for the legal services of Dawes, Walling, and about the prophecy that I'm going to commit a murder. Slowly but surely I am beginning to feel as if life is closing in on me and maybe I should buy that insurance policy in case I need legal services. But I don't say that to Trey. Instead, I'm thinking about this house: in the kitchen are the shiny appliances, and the food in its Tupperware containers, and out there in the living room are the comfortably worn-out brown sofa and the two matching chairs, and the pictures on the wall of Joe, Lena, Cheryl, and me, hanging near the bookcase, and, upstairs, my son and daughter and my daughter's boyfriend are doing whatever white midwestern American teenagers do, all these features of a calm and settled world, and I can hardly breathe as I think, *All this is temporary,* and my next thought is *My luck could run out, and all this could be taken away in a moment,* and I will be undone. I won't be myself anymore; I'll be stripped down, I'll have turned into someone else, someone I hardly know. If it happened to Job in the Old Testament, it could happen to anybody. *"Why is light given to him that is in misery?"* Job asks. Could be me. And my children—the children, including Pete—what will happen to them?

She nods. "You, a murderer? That's so preposterous. They don't know you, not the way I know you. Incidentally, I called the clinic today to ask them about Generomics. I felt I should, just in case. They said, and I quote, 'We regret our association with them, and beyond that, we have no comment.' No comment? That's what guilty people say, and it creeped me out, and next we'll be hearing them take the Fifth Amendment. It makes you wonder what other trouble Generomics got itself into."

"You mean, who else they suckered?"

"Yes, that's exactly what I mean." She pads out to the front of the house and comes back with the package delivered by UPS. "Okay, let's see what this is."

14

YOU ENTER THE KINGSBORO CONVALESCENT CARE FACILITY AND YOU
make your way toward the front desk decorated with a balloon
smiley face. That's the only smile you're going to see for the next
hour. They take your temperature, aiming this pistol-shaped
device at your forehead. The smell of spilled bodily fluids is in the
air. The grim receptionist receives you but does not welcome you.
You are simply another burdensome civilian visitor. After getting
the room number you need and signing in and putting on your
K95 mask as per instructions, you proceed down the hallway past
assorted human wreckage and their white-uniformed caretakers.
People who once looked like solid citizens—teachers, plumbers,
construction workers, file clerks—and who once paid taxes and
watered the garden and put out the trash and raised their children,
are now slumped in wheelchairs, all skin and bones, openmouthed
staring flesh lumps. Groaning, they reach for you, eager to convey
and to share their physical suffering. They look surprised that fate
hit them with the brass knuckles, the blackjack, and the monkey
fist. God apparently permits all this. But I don't believe it. The God
I love couldn't have engineered what I'm witnessing here. There
must be some other God also at work behind the scenes, a sub-
God, the mischief maker. From the rooms on either side of the
hallway come audible whimpers and moans of the accident-prone,

the senile, the misfortunate, and the discarded. All these sights and sounds are sobering, I guarantee.

The unregistered Finn 23 is in my car's trunk, unwrapped. Be patient. I'll get to that.

Down this same hallway, in a semiprivate room, lies Burt Kindlov, unmasked, in a hospital bed with raised rails on both sides. Near the corner, just under the window, my ex-wife, Cheryl, sits with a magazine in her lap. The wall-mounted TV is on but with the sound off. Burt's head is in an elaborate bandage, and he is attached at the arm, nose, and mouth to various hissing and gurgling tubes. He's not so handsome anymore. His body is deflating and his head is leaking. In the room you can hear the machines as they breathe in and out. After I enter, Cheryl closes the magazine, briefly straightens her hair as if for a social occasion, and says, without introduction, "How're we going to pay for this?"

"Good day to you, too. More to the point, how's Burt?" I ask. "What's his condition? Is he getting better?"

"Well, he's come out of his coma. His condition is stable. He's eating. He hasn't said anything yet. He may be deaf. He's a strong guy, in great physical shape, or at least he *was* before he fell down those stairs and hit his head, and the surgery. So maybe he'll recover. Who knows?"

"Poor guy."

"Your sympathy is arriving a little late."

"Cheryl, I didn't do this to him. Also, I'm here, aren't I? I've been praying for him."

"I'll bet you have. I'll bet you've been praying hard. We'll see what good *that* does. What've you told the kids? And I'm still asking: How're we going to pay for this?" She waits. "And the roof? What you gave me won't cover it."

I check out the TV: they're showing professional golf. The picture tube is worn out, so the grass on the links is blue. "The kids?

Lena and Joe haven't said much. I think Joe is mixed up about it, after being called a faggot and all, and feeling suicidal, but he's working out with weights in the basement, did you know that? Those barbells you bought him? So *he's* okay. I think he feels bad for Burt, sort of, maybe. Somehow. Like something he set into motion. Lena hasn't said anything."

"Uh-huh," she says. "She called me and texted me. Said she'd be there for me if I needed her. I wish I knew what that meant. I hate that phrase, 'be there for you.'" She asks me again about how we're going to pay for this.

"What's this 'we'?" I'm looking around for another chair, but there isn't one.

"You. Me. Us."

"I don't think there's an Us. Burt never bothered to marry you. You and he weren't legally a team."

"So what happens with the medical bills?" she asks me. She's sounding desperate.

"I suggest prayer."

"This is no time for irony," Cheryl says. "You can't imagine how expensive all this is."

"Yes, I can. Medical bills are my business. Sorry. But I sort of meant it, about prayer."

Cheryl sits up. I can tell from her face that she's been crying, and I think: *What have I done?* I have a sudden memory of when I used to love her. I have one of those flash memories of our honeymoon: meals together, quiet and sometimes noisy lovemaking. But now she sticks out her index finger to make a point. "Well, so, yeah. So what about his parents? His father's dead. Burt's mother and her boyfriend moved to Montana, and they live on Social Security in a little cottage outside of Billings. No savings, they tell me—they spent it all on the nice little cottage. And the garden! They grow turnips. Zucchini, squash, the slum vegetables. Good for them. Told me to keep them *updated* about Burt, like he's an offspring blip on their radar screen. *We've never been close,* his mother tells me. They aren't coming here, not yet. Can you imagine? His sister's a meth-head-plus-heroin-addict living in Westerville. She's out of jail now, but *that* won't last. He doesn't have kids, obviously. And *somebody's* got to pay for this. The officials've been asking me about it. The questions are getting more urgent. The money collectors have been quite irritable over the phone. The sums of money they're talking about! And seizing assets, garnishing wages, et cetera. They've even suggested that they might put him out into the street, bedridden and all. He didn't have any medical insurance—he never signed up. Typical. Burt always thought he was indestructible. And he was, for a while. His mother and her boyfriend have disclaimed any financial responsibility. Real sweethearts, those two."

"He *did* fall off that roof. Doesn't he qualify for Medicaid?"

"I've been reading the Ohio Medicaid website. Unbelievable. It's unintelligible. But I think he qualifies, though maybe only after they've seized his savings and our house, which is in his name. I guess I've got to talk to someone who knows about these forms." Cheryl's voice sounds funny when filtered through the mask, like that former movie star Ethel Merman.

"Not to change the subject, but I'm not here to offer advice about that. Although I could."

"What *are* you here for?"

"I'm here for what you're here for."

"Which is?"

"Look, Cheryl," I say, and then I tell her that I'm sorry about what's happened to Burt, and I say that I'm sorry that she's angry at me but that I'll do my best to help sort out the medical bills— yes, I do have some expertise with such matters—but that I honestly didn't like Burt and never have, and after all she did run off with him, and I think he's a sponge and a narcissist and a creep, but he's a fellow human being, a child of God, and I'm here at the Kingsboro Convalescent Care Facility out of respect for him and for her, because she loves him, after all.

"That's where you're wrong," she says in a neutral tone, opening the magazine in order to pretend to read an article. "I don't love him. I never did."

"You didn't?"

"No."

"Then why'd you run off with him?"

"He was more interesting than you." She's not looking up at me. "That's all. Burt was more interesting." Now she does look up. "He was never boring."

15

PEOPLE DIVIDE OUR FELLOW AMERICANS IN VARIOUS WAYS, INTO CAT-
egories, like sports teams: North versus South; Republican or
Democrat; straight or gay; an ethnic identity like White or Black
or some other racial classification; country versus city; college
education versus just high school or less; men versus women
versus nonbinary; old versus young; cool versus uncool, and of
course I'm forgetting some of the other divisions, those versuses
that separate us and put us into the pigeonholes where the pigeons
are. People love these divisions, can't get enough of them. *You're
not like me? Fuck you!* That's the logic. Some of those pigeonholes
are ones we ourselves have chosen, and the other pigeons were not
of our own making. Fate tells us who we are before we've made
up our minds on the subject.

I was trying to figure out what new category I had fallen into,
and the one I settled on was this: *I have turned into someone who
keeps a loaded handgun in the bedroom.* Many fine Americans, my
brothers and sisters in this our life, perfectly decent people and
solid citizens, put their trust in the police and don't keep loaded
handguns in the bedside table's drawer. I never used to, but I do
now, and that distinction separates me from the unarmed. I now
own a first-class, top-of-the-line Finn 23. Generomics sent it to me,
along with bullets, in a package with no return address deposited

on my doorstep. You could call it encouragement, like a cherry bomb and a match in the hands of a sixth-grade boy.

I have figured those Generomics characters out. They are tempters intent on doing harm, as performed by me and others, and they will profit from my efforts at crime. It's in their interests financially for me to shoot somebody. New frontiers in capitalism are always opening up when you think nothing new is on the horizon. I just haven't quite figured out exactly where and how they'll make money from my misdeeds, but it's plain that they will, somehow. Kickbacks from the lawyers, maybe. Privatized, for-profit prisons, that sort of thing. The market for murder is an expanding field where the sun shines all day long.

BY NOW YOU MIGHT HAVE STARTED TO WONDER WHAT KIND OF COMpany Generomics is: who runs it, how they make money, where their laboratories are housed, what sorts of liabilities they might have, and whether their blood test has any scientific validity whatsoever. These are questions that I should have thought about sooner. I was so excited by their promise of predicting my future that I didn't bother researching them with due diligence. You don't usually ask the soothsayers or the psychics where they went to high school or whether they had happy childhoods or when and how they lost their virginity. Some things you just have to take on faith. I am a man of faith. But criminals, I have learned, are faithless.

The next day I was on the phone, trying to get a number for Generomics in Cambridge, Massachusetts. No number was listed. I went to their nonexistent website: it still refused to exist. I fished out the business card that Alan Pilensky gave me, but the phone number on it was bogus, as was the email address. When I called the Kingsboro Medical Clinic, they told me exactly what they told Trey: that they had severed all relations with Generomics and that they regretted any attachment they had once had to the blood test I had taken, and, they quickly added, they were not liable. *Extremely* not liable. I was the one who had signed on the dotted line. "We're sorry," they said, "but not *totally* sorry. We were misled and misinformed. There was some human error. We meant well. However, now you're on your own. You might call the Better Business Bureau. We're not responsible."

Generomics gave me a ladder onto the roof, and then once I was up there, they kicked away the ladder. Sometimes I think a good-sized minority of our fellow citizens are plotting similar scams. It beats working.

Nevertheless, I had filled out the insurance application from Glickman-Doerr and had mailed it along with a check, so presumably I was now covered and protected by those ankle-biting lawyers at Dawes, Walling. I had checked them out; they existed, just as I had been informed. Lucky me! Those white-shoe members of the bar had my back.

And so, thus armed and insured with protective services—I was beginning to think of them as my bodyguards—and under a cloud of prophecy that claimed I was about to become a murderer, I went back to my life, a life as ordinary and as calm as a lake that you discover after a long hike in the wilderness—a lake that isn't on your map and doesn't have a name or a fixed location but whose surface reflects the blue sky, and, until you get there and dip your hands in the water, is untouched.

Part II

Please follow me because I have
to follow him and he isn't here.

—Eugene Ormandy

16

WHEN YOU REALIZE THAT YOU'RE THE VICTIM OF AN ELABORATE SCAM, you can be either angry or ashamed of yourself. If you're feeling shame for being conned, you're a fool, and you therefore keep your mouth shut so as not to reveal your fool-identity and how brazenly stupid you were. Generomics never existed except as a carnival sideshow, even though the people in our local clinic briefly believed that it was legit. Anyway, the point is, I'd been fooled and swindled, and I went on with my life.

I helped Cheryl out with the medical bills and arranged for Burt, the invalid, to go on Medicaid. I'm a bureaucrat at heart, so it wasn't that difficult. There were copays, bills with deadlines, and I helped out with that. I didn't feel guilty about Burt's condition, but I didn't feel like an innocent bystander, either.

Therefore, I went back to check on him a couple of times at the Kingsboro Convalescent Care Facility, and as the days went on, he seemed to be returning to this world, this life. No more respirator. He was eating with assistance, his eyes had opened, and he seemed—*seemed!*—to be concentrating on somebody or something in front of him, not the TV, but a presence coming out of the wall that faced his bed. His mouth would open, but no sounds came out. This was not disappointing. Stringy hair and dead eyes: he was beginning to look like the panhandlers he hated. He could sometimes communicate with yes-or-no eyeblinks or finger taps, one blink for yes, two blinks for no. God only knows what condition his mind was in or what was passing through that ill-furnished locale as the days passed. They told me his thinking might well be impaired, and I resisted the easy wisecrack about Burt's thinking, such as it was, prior to his fall.

Cheryl's visits were periodic. I surmise that she wasn't prepared for Burt to be an invalid or to look the way he did now. She had an idea of him, and this wasn't it. A few of Burt's other friends—he didn't have many of them, a mere handful if a couple of your fingers had been amputated—showed up and then quickly disappeared. Guys like that are afraid of hospitals, and they're useless when it comes to comforting the sick. So I was there alone with him when he first spoke. I'd been listening to his usual nonsensical verbal noises, when after turning his head and seeing me, he said with shocking clarity, "Oh it's you." Immediately I went out to the hallway and called for a nurse to witness Burt's return to the world of intelligible words and syntax from the nonsensical Lotusland he'd been inhabiting.

Three days later when I again stopped by his room, Cheryl still wasn't there. Sleet was falling from a pug-ugly sky and pinging against the window, a harbinger of midwinter. With the tip of his tongue protruding from his mouth like a lizard waiting for a fly, Burt sat in the chair next to the heating outlet, and, dressed in hospital attire, he conveyed through looks alone a change in personality, which is to say that I couldn't tell whether he was still himself or whether his fall had taken him to another plane of existence and converted him into a kindly invalid. Fat chance! He peered quizzically at the doorway when I entered, as if the room's walls were disfigured with nasty graffiti commentary about him that needed deciphering. With his head cocked to one side he also gave the impression that he was listening to voices or music that no one else could hear. Maybe it was the mind-frazzle of the drugs.

Maybe he was high and had seen the nothingness at the heart of things and become a Buddhist. When people are hospitalized, they don't always notice what's going on next to them. Burt had never been the most observant guy or the sharpest knife in the drawer anyway, so why would he be different now? A skull fracture would not brighten his dim bulb. I know that sounds mean, but so what? I never liked him. I didn't like him when we were in first grade together and I didn't like him now. Anyway, I was standing near him trying to master my loathing of the guy and then sat down in the visitor's chair they had finally found somewhere and put in this room. When I sat, the cushion wheezed and exhaled.

Most hospital rooms have flowers. This one didn't. Flowers signify love. Burt was at the other end of that particular spectrum.

To answer your question, I'm not sure why I kept going back to see him. Most men would not. Even the greatest saints would have stayed away. Saint Ignatius of Loyola would not have bothered to visit Burt in the hospital. Mother Teresa would have found better things to do. But I had a nagging sense that he and I had some unfinished business to attend to.

What do you say to such a person at such a time? "Burt," I asked, "how are you?"

"Who you?"

"Brock," I said. "Brock Hobson. I used to be married to Cheryl."

"Who Cheryl?"

"You live with her. She's your girlfriend. My ex-wife."

"Oh okay. Um. Yeah."

I waited. He seemed ready, ripened, to make an acute observation about how he felt and what his condition was. "So how're you doin'?" I asked. "How do you feel?"

"Pain. Pain been taking me to lunch. Using me for spare parts."

"Taking what? Who's been taking?"

"The doctors."

"What have they taken?"

"Me. My insides."

"Care to explain?"

"Took my heart. Cut me open and took it. Haven't got one now."

"No kidding. Your actual heart? The cardiac muscle?"

"Took it away. Sold it in Mexico. Lungs too. Didn't ask me."

"They removed your lungs?"

"Yep. Can't breathe no more."

"Why'd they take them?" I asked.

"Selling them off. Wanted them," he said. "For sale. Discount. Took my kidneys."

"What for?"

"Don't know."

And now comes the painful part of my story, the part I would rather not tell. But a storyteller is bound to the truth. Fair warning: Dear reader, if you have made it this far in my story, I would advise you to hold on to the sides of your chair because of what Burt then said in response to my next question.

"*Who* took your heart?"

"The doctors. The ▮▮▮ doctors. ▮▮▮▮▮▮▮▮▮▮" I am redacting what he actually said to protect you, dear reader, and your more delicate feelings. Burt shouldn't have access to a microphone and a public address system.

I felt myself getting very cold, freezing up. "Burt, you can't say that. You *can't say that.* And it didn't happen."

"Just said it."

"It's crazy. And it's not true."

"Saw it. Swear to God."

"You saw it?"

"Eyes open alla time. Me, on a table. Them, with knives. Cutting into me. Takin' everything I got: heart, lungs, all of it."

"You were hallucinating."

"I was hell-ucinating. In Hell. They cut you open, take what they want. In Hell, it's theirs. They got you into little pieces. You just a junkyard to them. For spare parts. Then they sew you up."

At that point, he leaned back and closed his eyes.

"You're imagining things," I said.

"Nope. Big room. People watching everything. They got knives. Cutting me, guts for sale. I couldn't move. You too. You didn't stop them. They leaned down ███████████████████ ███████████████████████████████████████ ███████████████████████████████████████ ███████████████████████████████████████."

The effort to speak seemed to tire him out, and he closed his eyes.

"Burt, you were dreaming."

"Then my bones. Stripped me clean. Flaying me. For cat food. Fucking *cats*!"

"You were dreaming."

"But the dreams was real."

Well, I suppose he was delirious. And a brain injury can take away your inhibitions, they tell me. People say that when you're delirious, you're not yourself. But when Burt was delirious, he was much more himself than usual, more fully opinionated. His evil egg had hatched, and this shadowy arachnid thing came out. Therefore, I got up and left. Let the son of a bitch take care of his own hospital bills.

Where was my Finn 23? I too am not a paragon of virtue: I might've shot him there and then if I had been someone else and not the person I imagine myself to be.

17

THE CHILDREN IN MY SUNDAY SCHOOL CLASS ALWAYS WANTED TO HEAR about Christ's crucifixion, the nails especially (how deep they went, and what they were made of), the spear in the side, the blood and the wounds, and instead I always wanted to teach them about the Sermon on the Mount. Forgiveness, love, kindness, charity—those enemies of juicy stories. I wanted to teach those kids about loving your enemies, but this bored or baffled them, and when I talked about these virtues, down there in the church basement near the kitchen, where the faucet dripped relentlessly into the sink, their eyes got glassy, and they yawned.

But when I explained to them about the resurrection and the wounds, they perked up.

I'd been talking about the Gospel of Luke and its ending when Billy Tarbox, who was sitting near the end of the rectangular table where we were gathered, raised his hand. He had a round face and glasses, and his uncombed hair made him look like the "before" ad for kids' hair spray. Still, he was a sweet kid with a heroic single-parent mom who had two other kids, one of them grown and in the Army and off drugs by now. "Yes, Billy?"

"The way you're talking about Jesus, he sounds like a super-hero. He sounds just like Voltrano. Was Jesus like some avatar for Voltrano? It sounds like it."

"No. Who's Voltrano?"

"He's this superhero guy who was, like, born on another planet, Agaragar, where they also had the star over Bethlehem except it was over Blorgon, and he came here and died, and then some other Agaragarians came in a ship and, like, brought him back to life so he could fight the evil Blorgons, who live underground in the Cobalt Cave." He waited for my response. "They had killed him with plutonium death rays because of how good and kind he was, and he was going to save the Morpheans. The Blorgons hate the Morpheans, who're led by Morax, who's so totally bad, nobody could be worse." This made him smile. "Morax doesn't take baths, and he eats by sucking bone marrow. So he's, like, also disgusting besides being superbad."

I tried to think of what to say. "That's not the same thing," I told him. "Christ healed the sick and raised the dead and was resurrected after he was crucified." I smiled. "And he really existed. He was the Son of God."

"Okay, yeah," Billy said, "but there are no movies of him. Or videos. So how can you, like, prove it? And anyway Voltrano did all that. Except he wasn't crucified. With him it was plutonium death rays from the Death Generator deep inside the Cobalt Cave, like I said. Plus he had superpowers. He can, like, walk on water if he wants to, and fire doesn't burn him because he can talk to it, and he can make fire turn into rain." As an afterthought, he said, "And sometimes he can fly. When he has his gold ring that the wizard gave him after the Five Trials. You don't get the gold ring unless you pass the Five Trials. Including the fiery furnace. Including the well of ghosts."

"That's imaginary," I said. "It's all made up. Where'd you read it?"

Another boy, Jake Goetz, raised his hand. "Mr. Hobson, Voltrano wasn't born on Agaragar. Voltrano was born on Blissarion. Morax was born on Agaragar. Billy's confused. Morax is totally

evil—if he smiles at you, you die on account of his electric eyes."
At this, Billy Tarbox shook his head and crossed his arms. The
three girls in class began to signal their impatience. "You've got
your planets mixed up," Jake concluded. "Blissarion is where the
Morpheans live in the Ice Galaxy."

Then Sally Horns spoke up. "Mr. Hobson, how come Jesus
forgave everybody? In the Bible it says he cursed a fig tree and it
died. It withered up. So he didn't forgive *everything*. He could get
mad. And the Bible is not like Miracle Comix, you guys. You're
such . . ." She didn't finish her sentence. The boys in class smirked
at her. "You're such *weirdos*," she finally said, and their smirks disappeared. The boys were all sitting on one side of the table, and
the girls were massed on the other side. "You guys are all out in
outer space," she said, staring at them as a group. "Boys are *so*
stupid."

This made Tommy Edie raise his hand. He had been following the conversation with deep concentration. "Yeah, but at least
we're not talking about princesses and castles and unicorns all the
time. Unicorns aren't real! So was Jesus, y'know, the first superhero?" He was asking me, but the other kids seemed interested in
the question. "Because most of what the Bible says about him is
what superheroes do, except the forgiveness part. They don't get
to forgive anybody, and they don't want to, except their friends
sometimes, like before a battle when they need help."

A girl sitting next to Sally Horns, Stella Crane-Randolph, who
always wore the same pink barrettes and who had matching pink-
frame glasses with thick lenses in front of her watery blue eyes,
raised her hand and said simultaneously, "You didn't answer Sally's
question. I don't get why a person has to forgive everybody. Just
because the Bible says it? I don't get that. My mom doesn't forgive
people. And she's my mom. She has . . . I can't think of the word."

"Grudges?" I suggested.

"Yeah, she's got those. Why's she supposed to forgive everybody?"

"Because—" I started to say, when the others all spoke up.

"Voltrano proves that payback is more fun than just sitting there," Tommy said, pulling at several strands of his hair. "Payback feels good. If you sit there while you get hit, it gets worse, and Morax comes at you with his blood-scoop, and if he misses you, his army of slave jackals gets set loose. And then *watch out*." He shook his head, but the thought of the jackals made him smile. He was happy. "They'll eat you. They're omnivores. So fighting back is better." He was saying all this while Jake Goetz was saying, "Jesus's disciples are just like Voltrano's buddy posse, except Voltrano had, like, only eight posse members: Sirissa and Bravearm and Blue Shirt and Bloodcurdle and—"

"Stop!" I said. "Wait!" But I could see that somehow a door had opened, and these kids had gone in through that doorway when pop-culture chaos had entered the room, and I would have to struggle to get them back out to reality. With great effort, I managed to return the discussion to the Bible and Jesus when Jake asked me, "Mr. Hobson, how come we're supposed to love our enemies?"

"Because Jesus did that. The Bible says so."

"Yeah, but it doesn't make any sense. How can you love someone you hate? Or can't stand?"

"You change your mind. It puts a stop to the mayhem."

"Yeah, but how?"

"I don't know. You just do it."

"I don't get it. Mr. Hobson, what's *your* superpower?"

"I don't have one."

"Everybody has a superpower. Jesus had a whole bunch of them. And you pray to him, right? Like we're supposed to? You don't have to be a superhero to have a superpower."

"No," I said. "I'm an ordinary person."

"Are you sure?" he asked. "People say they're ordinary, and it turns out they're always wrong."

"Really?" I said. "Do *you* have a superpower, Jake?"

He nodded. "Yeah. But I'm not supposed to tell."

"Who says so? But maybe you could tell *us*."

"Nope. But you're a grown-up, and you teach Sunday school, like now. In Miracle Comix it says most people have a superpower, only sometimes they don't know what it is. Or maybe they don't care or they gave up years ago, or they have a superpower and don't use it. Sometimes you need a wise old wizard to tell you what your superpower is."

"I don't have a wise old wizard in my life," I told him. "I never have." I was going to play the grump. "I don't even know what a wizard looks like."

"Maybe he looks like you. C'mon," Billy Tarbox said. He had raised his arms to stretch. "What would your kids say your superpower is?"

"I told you. They'd say I don't have one."

As one, all the boys and girls said, "*C'mon.*"

"I'm ordinary," I said. "One of God's creatures."

Stella Crane-Randolph said, "No one is ordinary. Everyone is someone *special.*"

"Not me," I said.

"But if you were a character in Miracle Comix, what would they say your superpower is?"

I waited there, with the sound of the dripping water faucet on the other side of the church basement. Outside, the wind was making a racket, and I could almost hear the ticking of my wristwatch. Sometimes, without your knowing it, time stops, and everyone freezes in place in their settled positions, and you are being put to a test, and time won't start up until you've passed the exam and said what needs saying. If you don't say it, you'll be frozen there for life.

"I think I can raise the dead," I told them, and some of them made an effort to smile while the others frowned. "I just haven't tried to do it yet."

Well, that stopped them. Besides, strictly speaking, it wasn't true. I had already brought one person back to life.

It had just come out of my mouth. I hadn't meant to say it; it just came out.

18

GENEROMICS'S PREDICTIONS ABOUT MY BEING A MURDERER, AND Burt's skull fracture and hospitalization, and the way the kids in my Sunday school class had acted—all these events put me under what many people would call stress. I felt like an old rusting bridge over which a heavy truck was crossing, making the supports creak and shudder. Once these troubles entered my life, my chest knotted up, and I noticed that I was hearing oddball sounds, like birds chirping inside my office near the heat ducts. I couldn't sleep. The loaded Finn 23 was stashed in the drawer of my bedside table, and at night I saw strange patterns on the bedroom ceiling, including animals that did not exist in nature. I felt that these animals wanted to speak to me, to pass on, in confidence, their plans of action, along with personal advice.

Days passed, and for some reason, one that I could not clearly define for myself or anyone else, I began to limp. There was no reason for it. I just had it. A kind of secret intermittent pain, which I have to compare to a long-distance telephone call from an anonymous insane person with a hidden agenda, was afflicting my left knee and hip, and other parts of my body seemed to be sending me signals that something was terribly wrong. It wasn't so much *pain* pain as *wrong* pain, the pain you feel when your world is askew. I felt out of sorts, as if my body disagreed with me. A ringing like church bells—added to the hallucination sound of the birds—began in my ears, and in the afternoons I would doze off for no reason at my desk at the office, which had never happened to me before. (I wasn't sleeping at night, after all.) The skin around my ankles began to itch so severely that I felt they were on fire, and no lotions seemed to help. I was falling behind on insurance work, and my assistants had to take up the slack. My backaches started up again (sciatica? or the weight of the world on my shoulders?), and I acquired a stoop-shouldered walk. People seeing me bent over like that were alarmed, hurrying up to me with sympathetic clucks, and one of my friends, seeing me out on the sidewalk in downtown Kingsboro, said to me, "What happened to you? You look diminished."

Diminished! When I went to the clinic, they ran the usual tests on me, and when the test results came back, my usual doctor, Evelyn Curtis, MD, came into the consulting room and said to me, "Brock, nothing has shown up here. All the blood test results are well within the usual norms."

"What about the unusual norms?" I asked.

"Those too," she said with a benevolent smile, meant to put me at ease. "I wouldn't worry if I were you. You're as fit as a fiddle. I wonder why people say that about fiddles? Anyway, except for the fact that you're feeling these pains, and you complain that you can't breathe and you've lost your appetite and there's a tightness in your chest, and you feel like you're dying, you're fine. Those symptoms are troublesome, however. They are warning signs. So are the auditory hallucinations and the panic attacks. No one wants to feel the way you do. It's not an ideal somatic situation. You know," she told me, leaning toward me from her chair in front of her computer screen, "just because a pain is psychosomatic doesn't mean it isn't real. It's as real as any other kind of pain."

As she said this, my nose spontaneously began to bleed. "Well, by golly," she said, "would you look at that. Here." She handed me a tissue, which I balled up and stuffed into my nostril.

"Do you habe any adwice?" I asked her, holding my head tilted back. With my nose stuffed with Kleenex, the words came out sounding clotted and European.

"Maybe you should go away for a while," she suggested, as the blood from my nostril soaked the tissue implanted there. "Hawaii is nice. Beaches. Active volcanoes. Sunshine. Pacific Ocean breezes. Get away from the winter blahs. I also have a psychiatrist I can recommend, Dr. T. D. Bowen. Deet—that's his nickname. Deet is very good, if you want his help. He's a virtuoso of the prescription pad. He'll give you drugs no one else has ever heard of."

"Isn't Deet a mosquito repellant? Is this guy a shrink?"

"We don't call them that anymore."

"But that's what he is. Doctor, I'm not crazy."

"I didn't say that you were." She continued to smile at me in a friendly way, but you could tell that she had other patients to get to and wanted to finish up with me. It was what you'd call an impatient smile with a micro-hint of downbeat irritation. Doctors have rigid schedules to adhere to. Insurance firms insist on that. Her face was a barometer and not that hard to read. "Sanity has a wide spectrum. You should learn to relax. Do you play basketball? Do you swim at the Y? Do you have hobbies? A lot of people enjoy collecting stamps or taking long walks, or they sign up for ballroom dancing. And how about swing dancing? That's a *great* stress reliever. And it's fun! You throw your partner around. Or you could learn a foreign language at Kingsboro Community College. You could sprechen Sie Deutsch. The world," she said, sounding like a middle school guidance counselor trying to prevent suicide attempts, "is full of wonderful activities."

"I sense that you're grasping at straws," I said. "But I do

appreciate your efforts." I took the old tissue out of my nostril and inserted another one. A drop of my blood landed in my lap before I could daub it away, staining my khakis. People are quick to notice bloodstains on your clothes, as a rule. They're giveaways to all other kinds of unpleasantnesses. Meanwhile, Dr. Curtis—I had once called her Evelyn and she had given me a dirty look, so I never did that again, having learned that doctors are deeply invested in their own importance and don't care for familiarity from their patients—fetched her prescription pad and wrote out an Rx for Rezillify.

"This might calm you down," she said, ripping the sheet off the pad. "But don't take these pills habitually and don't drink at the same time. They can knock you out flat. And they're slow to metabolize. I don't want to find you at the ER. I don't want to hear that you've died."

"Or that I've murdered someone?"

"That, too," she said. "Why do you say that?"

I didn't want to go into the whole Generomics misadventure, so I said, "Oh, I didn't mean anything by it." She nodded. "Thank you, Doctor," I said, taking the prescription from her hand.

"Take care, Brock," she said. "If you have any more hallucinations, give the office a call. Mind how you go."

A British expression! I wonder where she got it from.

OUR HOUSEHOLD RESUMED ITS USUAL ROUTINES, WITH THE ADDITION of Bobby the rat, who was doted on by both Joe and Lena, who carried him around the house (the rat's favorite perch was the top of Joe's head, where he clung to Joe's hair and scalp) and brought him to the dinner table, though I drew the line at having him scampering around from one salad plate to another, snacking on leftovers. I don't care how companionable or clean white rats are;

they're still rats. It didn't look good, having a rat on the table at mealtime. The rat's run of the crockery and silverware suggested that ordinary standards of sanitation were not being observed. I should mention that around then, after Thanksgiving, Joe's suicidal notes also stopped, as did his various despairs, now that Burt was semi-muzzled by his injuries. I still heard the clanking of Joe's barbell equipment in the basement, however, as he huffed and puffed his way through his workouts toward his goal of looking like Adonis. Lena and Pete turned in their college applications as the dreaded holiday season descended, and so far I hadn't killed anyone, as had been predicted by the algorithms. I noticed, as the winter gained momentum, that Lena and Pete's passion for each other seemed to be diminishing, and though their fire had not been totally quenched, judging from the telltale banging of the headboard, the sound was less fervent and more subdued, almost domestic. They were getting more and more like a married couple. I did not comment on that, though it brought a wry sadness into my heart.

As for Burt and my ex-wife, they were on the horizon, cooking up various storms, speaking of barometers.

Sometimes I would excuse myself from the office, claiming to my assistants that I was out on business, and instead of doing any sort of commercial transaction I would drive to Knoblauch County Park, partly because Trey worked there and partly because my nerves were shot. I'd go into the interpretive center, where she worked, and she'd give me a loving peck on the cheek, and I'd admire her in her green park uniform and the name tag and the jaunty hat with the wide brim, and sometimes I'd listen to her as she lectured the assembled fourth and fifth graders about foxes, owls, and snakes. Then I'd go out to the hiking trails—it's a large park, and some of the circle trails are three miles long—and do my best to get lost, to lose myself out there.

There's a story that I read in college that has stuck with me, even though I can't remember the author or the title of the story. It's about a man who one day leaves his wife and family, and the house where they all live, and he walks a block or so away and moves into a rented room with a window from which he can see his own house—who's coming and going. He stays in the rented room for days, weeks, months, years. He watches his wife entering and leaving the house. Does he still love her? The story refuses to say. (But how could he?) He sees how distraught she is at first, given his disappearance from her life, and then how quickly she seems to be aging, given his absence. Yet he does not return to his home. Time goes by, and—I think this is right—he even passes her on the street, and she doesn't recognize him. He's now a certified stranger. After decades, he leaves the rented room and returns to the house he had once abandoned. In the last line of the story, he goes in through the old familiar door. The author then calls him "the outcast of the universe." Even though the story is not plausible, it made a big impression on me. The best stories are the ones you almost can't believe because they're so true, the truth that surpasses plausibility.

That was how I was beginning to feel: that funny outcast sensation. The first few times I went to the county park, I walked down this path turning south, an old tree stump moldering on my left, and a bird feeder—no birds there—on my right, and slowly made my way to a little pond circled by cattails where geese and mallard ducks hung out, though at this time of year, with the temperatures falling, the geese were preparing to fly south and therefore had anxious and irritable demeanors like travelers in airports. The air was cold and damp, and you could perceive a muddy wildlife smell reeking of nitrogen. On two occasions I saw a muskrat crawl into a hut-like habitat, and on yet another walk I saw a raccoon ahead of me on the path, lumbering along like a little bear. Hearing me, it turned around and gazed at me without surprise before it ambled away. Exchanging a glance with this animal made me feel as if I hadn't completely severed my ties with daily life or with the natural order of things. I was grateful to that raccoon. Brother Raccoon, Sister Muskrat, how was your day?

All the same, what Generomics had done to me, combined with Burt's accident and the difficulties I had had with Joe, made me feel as if I had somehow broken away from my family, and my community, and the mysterious chain of being that ties us all together, if I could put it that way. I was out there floating in space, turning end over end, lost in my errant thoughts. So these walks I took in the county park reattached me to what was going on at ground level. That particular day I had brought some birdseed in my pocket, and when I arrived at a turn in the trail, near a cedar grove where I saw some chickadees, I put some seed in my palm and held my hand out flat, at shoulder level, and, sure enough, a brave chickadee flew down and picked and pocked at the seed before it flew away. Trey had fed wild animals, and now I could, too. Having a wild bird alight on your hand will take away your troubles for moments at a time, believe me. The few ounces of wildness in your hand are a visitation from the other world, the one that we know is there, which we can't see. There is another world and it's here, now. Wild animals can bring you evidence of that.

I continued on my walk. Up ahead near a very old maple tree whose branches appeared to be sagging from age, I saw a deer, a male—judging by his antlers—grazing on old grass, and I had expected the animal to run away in fright as they usually will, but this buck stood quite still after it raised its head, observing me, and it occurred to me that maybe he had the advantage: sharp hooves, bulk, and antlers. The deer was also in better physical condition than I was, given his daily exertions and his struggles for existence. As he stood there, he snorted. He had no interest in friendship between species. He distrusted humans, and for good reasons. At that moment I felt a tug at my sleeve: Trey, in her park ranger uniform, drawing me away from where I stood until we were a good half mile in the other direction. She must have been following me without telling me, as people will do when they start to worry about you.

"I was fine," I protested. "That deer had nothing on me."

"You're bluffing," she said. "If he had wanted to, he could have mowed you down."

"Is that the word?" I asked. "'Mowed'?"

"In your case, it is," she said. Right then I felt the warmth of her love for me, and on top of that particular feeling, I had a surge of gratitude that she had gone to the trouble to leave her post in the interpretive center to trail me, signifying her worries, but the moment was even larger than that: I felt gratitude (to her, to life) that she loved me and that I loved her, that it was reciprocal. I saw her graying hair underneath her cap, a sign that the clock was ticking for both of us. At that moment when we were both standing on the trail in the Knoblauch County Park on a gray overcast day, I asked her to marry me, and she accepted. I hadn't known that I was going to do that—I didn't have an engagement ring handy—but the realization had come to me that I wanted her in my life not temporarily but permanently, so I fashioned a little sprig of grass into a ring, tying the ends together with a tiny knot, and I put it on her finger, and she did her best to keep it there as we walked back. She was crying. I suppose I was, too.

19

WOMEN DON'T LIKE IT WHEN YOU MAKE GENERALIZATIONS ABOUT them. Everybody is someone special, they will say. However, I will be so bold as to assert that when you propose marriage and a life-long commitment to support and sustain one of them, the woman in question tends to receive the offer with sweet tenderness rather than scorn even if she ultimately rejects you. Women—here's another generalization again, go ahead, reader, sue me—love to be loved, whereas love, for many men, is often a pothole in the high-way of life. For many men, sexual attraction followed by marriage is the ultimate bait and switch. Furthermore, women are moved by professions of love even when they themselves are unable to return love in any of its forms. I am of course speaking hypothetically, but there was nothing hypothetical about my love for Trey or hers for me, or so it seemed, and we set a date for going to the courthouse to solemnize the nuptials. We did not plan to dress up for the occasion, but we did have to arrange the move of some of her belong-ings into my house, space being limited among the two teenaged children and Lena's (almost) live-in boyfriend, Pete, and what I assumed would be Joe's eventual introduction to me and everyone else of the first guy he would love and want to bring home. Life, in other words, was as complicated as ever, if not more so.

For the time being, Trey would keep her house and therefore

many of her belongings over there, with the house serving as a warehouse of her accumulations, but she would transfer her essentials (clothes, sewing machine, and knickknacks) to this house and to our spacious bedroom. We bought a dresser for her and put it near the bedroom window, and certain of her odds and ends found their way into the basement near the antique one-ton RCA color television and the antique Betamax tape player. By January we had worked out about 50 percent of what went where, and by the end of the month we were married. We hadn't eloped exactly, but given the way we did it, there were no fireworks, wedding toasts or speeches, drunkenness, dancing, rice throwing, one-night stands among the guests, or tin cans attached to the getaway car. We just said our vows before a witness and a judge, and we left the rest to circumstance. When you've got what we have, you don't need much ceremony.

Being married to Trey improved my mood (I didn't feel like an outcast anymore), and I had almost forgotten about Generomics and their predictions. But I hadn't forgotten about Burt Kindlov. I had wanted to, but fate wouldn't let me, so I couldn't. For one thing, I continued to send Cheryl money, even more money for the roof replacement that hadn't happened yet, and money for a healthcare professional who dropped in on Cheryl and Burt every few days to help in Burt's rehabilitation. If you are a successful insurance agent like me, trustworthy and decent, you can make a respectable living, but you can't support everybody in the world, particularly Cheryl and Burt, for whom I had small love and very little empathy and minimal interest. Also, I was anticipating the college expenses that Lena would incur next year as a freshman; even with a summer job and the part-time job to follow, once she enrolled, she would, I knew, come up short financially. I was watching my pennies, is what I'm saying.

. . .

I HAD NOT BEEN OVER TO CHERYL AND BURT'S HOUSE FOR A VISIT. Kingsboro is not a large community, and as a rule we are friendly and familial here, but after Burt's rant in the hospital, to say nothing of the way he had treated Joe, and the fact that he was living with my ex-wife, I didn't feel a single drop of the milk of human kindness, as it's called. Interesting that the expression includes the word "milk" and not "gasoline" or "olive oil." Why not the "water of human kindness"? I didn't feel any of those liquid things for Burt—just the opposite, in fact. Perhaps I felt the gasoline of antipathy. You could supply your own metaphors here.

So that was how things stood when the phone rang on a Saturday morning just before lunch. I took the call in the kitchen, and that landline does not happen to have caller ID, just my luck. It was Burt. "Is this you?" he asked. He has a slurry voice like a drunk disc jockey working past midnight, easy to recognize.

"Yes," I said. "Who's this?"

"This is Brock Hobson," he said.

"No, it isn't. Burt," I said, "you're confused. I'm Brock Hobson, not you."

"Oh? Is that right?" he asked. It sounded like "riiiiiaaaaaght." He was having a problem with vowels, to say nothing of his confusion of personal identities. I was interested that he thought he was me. "Who are you whatever to say who you are?" he asked nonsensically. "What gives you the riiiaaaght? Listen," he said. "I've got a thing or two to tell you, I've had time to think about it, you lousy son-of-a-bitch bastard. I've had a lotta time to think about you and what a piece-of-nothing shit you are, and a menace to society."

"Oh, really? What are your thoughts? Tell me." Sometimes you can't turn away from the bad movie, especially if it's about you.

Whereupon he launched into a largely unprintable tirade, using bits and pieces of R/Q Dynamics (including their fixation on lethargy-inducing plastic particles in our drinking water), along with other theories straight from "the Commandant" (R. Stan Drabble himself), and then veering off into a list of my personal failings that had something to do with how I had treated members of my family. Interspersed with these attacks on my character were his loathsome sidebar social commentaries, mostly about minorities. You can't reproduce his talk without being contaminated by it. I will therefore try to give the gist of what he said, while redacting the unprintable contents. You can imagine what's missing.

"You know who you remind me of?" he said, his voice sounding like an audible sneer. "You remind me of those ███████ who ██████ ██████ ██████ and just expect the ███████████████████, those dumb ████████████████████████. ████████████ ████████████ I misunderestimated you. You ████████████ are just dragging the country down, you and those ██—████ who never ████ and expect the ██████████████████████ to ████████████████. And something else: You know what Cheryl told me about you? She said that ██████████████████ and that ████████, and she said that you were so ████████ that she couldn't stand to ██████████████████ with you anymore. It's too bad that we're down on our luck and that I'm ████████████ on account of we still need that money to get by. I shoulda been friendly to you but I can't abide freakshow scum at the bottom of the ocean like yourself. It's not like ████████ like those ████████ ████████ and ████████ who never ██████████████████████. The Commandant talks about people like you, and he says—"

"Stop."

"██
and watch the elephant."

"Burt, stop it. It's the skull fracture talking."

"I'll show you skull fractures," he said, emboldened by his brain injury. "I'm going to come and get you and take what is legally mine. ██████████████████ You pushed me down those stairs and made me into the sorry person I am now."

"You shouldn't talk like this or say things like that to me. What's all this business of coming for me? You better watch yourself. Besides," I said, "I'd better warn you that I have a license to kill. I'm insured against everything. I'm insured against any harm I might do, I'm protected by those lawyers at Dawes, Walling. Didn't anyone tell you about the Generomics thing? Would you put Cheryl on the line? I need to talk to her."

"She ain't here. A license to kill? That's a good one. Suddenly you're James Fucking Bond. Double oh eight."

"It's double oh seven, Burt. Well, it's not quite like that, but it's similar."

At that point, he really got angry. His anger seemed genuine and sincere. "I've been listening to your stupid bullshit since first grade," he shouted, "and I'd rather eat a breakfast of bubble gum than spend another minute in your company."

"So hang up and calm down. Anyway, what's your beef with me?"

"Beef?"

"Yes. That's what I said."

"Beef?" He seemed unable to process the metaphor. "You . . . it ain't a beef, it's more like I can't stand you."

"So it seems we're at an impasse."

"No, we ain't."

"How much money are you asking for this time?" I queried.

"All of it."

"Now you're being silly. You want all my money?"

"That's it, that's what I said. That's my dough. The damages. And I'm gonna get it, too."

"Well, you can't have it. It's not yours. Besides, it's in the bank."

"Okay, get this. When I was unconscious, you know, hooked up to those machines? I saw you, like in a coma, where . . . and I saw God and Satan too, and they was the same? That was a big-time surprise. Better not tell anybody. But my point is, I saw you, and I learned the truth from them. That truth you been hiding all this time."

"Which is?" I was humoring him.

"You are totally made of plastic. Top to bottom. You are a replica human being."

"Not that again."

"And you was the person taking out my heart so you could have one of your own, and my skin and bones, and my inner organs, so you could be a human person. Instead of the plastic nonperson that you are."

"What is this you're talking about?" I asked. "Getting a heart? Isn't that the Cowardly Lion? *The Wizard of Oz?* Really? Or . . . what? Maybe *Pinocchio?*"

"What're you sayin'?"

"This conversation is over," I told him.

"You ain't real. You're like what they call an optical illusion. I figured it all out. The dream showed me. You ain't a real person, just a pretend person. I'm comin' for you. I'm gonna ███████████ ██████████████████████████████████████ ██ ██ ██████████████████████████ so called. That's my alibi. Then I'll take the money, the damages. Which is mine by rights. I don't even need a lawyer, like you got."

"Goodbye. I've heard enough."

"Bottom line, I'ma comin' for you. I got a hammer and you're the nail. When I get finished with you, you gonna wish you was in a snuff film, compared to."

"Good luck with that. Last I heard, you were on crutches. You're going to hobble over here?"

"Bottom line, I'm coming for you."

"You said that already. Bring it on."

20

A BIT LATER, CHERYL CALLED TO APOLOGIZE. "BURT ISN'T HIMSELF," she informed me. "It's not him who called you but . . . I mean, yes, it *was* him, but with his fall and the skull fracture, he's been through some hard times. Please forgive him. He's sorry he made that call. His accident changed his personality so he's mostly unrecognizable."

"Unrecognizable? *I* recognized him," I said. "Did you hear what he said to me? His last phone call? He threatened me."

"No, I was upstairs, changing the sheets." She let out a little half-sob. "I have to do that every day. Our washing machine gets quite a workout. It's been pretty difficult around here, with Burt the way he is, leaking and stuff. He can hardly get to the bathroom by himself. They told me that his brain injury would make him disinhibited, but I didn't know what that word meant until he came home and started talking. He curses at me, really bad language, unspeakable except he speaks it. If he were capable of hitting me, he probably would. Oh, I almost forgot: Congratulations. I heard you married Gertrude."

"You can call her Trey. Everyone else does. Thanks."

"You're welcome. Anyway, please don't blame me for what Burt is saying. I really don't know what to do. I can't abandon him like this. I mean, he's a mess. He doesn't look like himself. He doesn't even look like anybody."

I was about to say, "I'm sorry," but I wasn't sorry, so I couldn't say it.

"Oh, and about the money," she said, and then came the ask.

READER, IT'S JUST POSSIBLE THAT AS A TRUE-BLUE AMERICAN, YOU ARE knowledgeable about firearms, their use and misuse. And so it's also quite likely that you are familiar with the Finn 23. As I learned from YouTube presentations and from what Rogelio (a friend of mine from church, where he is a deacon) told me at his gun shop a mile outside of Kingsboro, the number 23 has nothing much to do with anything. The uninitiated might assume that the numeral 23 located after the brand name refers to caliber or some such thing. But no: "23" is simply the model number, whereas the actual caliber of the gun is nine millimeters, or, as the techies like to say, 9 x 19mm. (You can look up the Finn on the internet for more information, if you're curious, as some of you are likely to be. I'll wait here until you come back.) These are technicalities, but many of you gun fanciers will know what I'm talking about. The magazine of the Finn 23 contains seventeen bullets. The gun is equipped with a compact slide. It's probably a rip-off of the more expensive Glock 45. What else do you need to know? I won't bother with more details. You can look it up.

Now that I was a gun owner and was being threatened by a lunatic, I figured it was time to get some target practice. On a Saturday in February I took the Finn and several loaded magazines that I'd bought at Rogelio's gun shop, and I drove out to Eben Sharib's firing range. Eben (short for "Ebenezer," I believe, a somewhat antique name from the Bible, as in 1 Samuel 7:12) has a farm outside of Kingsboro along County Highway 14b, and he has both an indoor and an outdoor range set up to make a little extra money. There are quite a few gun enthusiasts in Kingsboro, so you have to make an appointment to get some shooting time. Eben's a nice guy—he's bought and renewed several fire-and-water-damage policies from me over the years—and though he's a little tattered as a human being, wounded in some obscure manner, he masks it quite well by wearing a big hat everywhere he goes, rain or shine.

When I got there, Eben took it upon himself to instruct me in the use of the Finn 23, and before you could say Jack Robinson, I was on the firing range, shooting at a target twenty-eight feet away. He had asked me whether the gun was registered, and I said, "Yup," and whether I had a conceal-and-carry permit, and I said, "Uh-huh," and he said, "Just checking." The kick of the Finn wasn't too bad, and before long I was getting the knack of it. Eben had outfitted me with Berman-Heffelfinger No-Sound™ ear protection—those over-the-ear things that look like head-phones—so I wouldn't blow out my eardrums shooting the Finn, and he also equipped me with goggles, to protect my eyes for some reason about which I won't speculate, and after a period of time that seemed to fly by, minutes that passed like mere seconds, I was shooting with a considerable degree of accuracy and further-more was getting a charged-up feeling that I had never experienced before in my life, except maybe in the moments before I first made love to Cheryl after the senior prom. (Backseat, my dad's car, and, as I remember, quick.) I am compelled to say that the Finn made me experience the joy of a conqueror, a potent man of action who was almost if not quite invulnerable. My blood began to surge, to heat up. It was elemental and furnace-like. I felt the heat in my chest and thighs and in my balls, even in my hands, almost (you could say) as if I were transforming myself, de-virginizing myself with the aid of the Finn 23, into a different man altogether, some-one who didn't take orders but gave them out, a commander. I'm talking about power and consequence and invulnerability. I was growing bigger, stronger than I had ever been. Laugh if you must. Anything I had ever feared began to fall away, as if the Finn had given to me an insurance policy that could never be canceled as long as I had another magazine full of bullets.

I'm a Sunday school teacher, so I have to say that I was surprised by this outcome. I thought I knew myself fairly well, but this sudden power felt like a narcotic, except that I was not in a heroin lotus haze but its opposite, a powerful (I keep using that word) alpha male awakening in which I was fearless, a victor, a subjugator, no longer cowering in fear—if I ever did—but standing up tall and strong, a man to contend with. This was real insurance. The other kind, which I sold, was little pieces of paper.

Who could have predicted this?

DAY BY DAY, AT THE OFFICE, AT MY DESK, I FELT THE NEED TO GET outside. I wanted to be a hunter, an adversary, a person to be reckoned with, one of those alpha and apex types, though I didn't exactly want to kill anything; I wouldn't go that far. I began to experience my own office as a drab, comfortable chicken coop of nothingness where no events of any importance had taken place or would ever take place. Chickens came and went. (I could recognize that my new mood was not good for business and verged on being inappropriate.) I would gaze out the window at the boring snow falling on the tedious streets and mind-numbing sidewalks where sad, dreary, unemployed fellow citizens were buying meth and cocaine in order to feel a little better about their stupid pointless lives. I had the cure for those feelings.

I was a changed man, is what I'm saying. For once in my life I felt that the proposition *life = suffering* was mistaken. If there was to be suffering, it would not be mine.

One afternoon I snuck out of the office and drove half an hour over to the Ringer County Wilderness Park, feeling the need to shoot something, though not to kill it, as I said. The park is not entirely a wilderness. Don't be misled. It has shelters and trails. The Ringer Park consists of about four thousand acres of wooded land, Ohio's answer to New Jersey's Pine Barrens, with rocky outcroppings and streams and thick undergrowth and two lakes fed by natural springs. You *could* get lost in there if you really tried to evade capture, and in bad weather you could suffer exposure and die if you set your mind to self-fatality, but there are ranger stations at the roadside when you enter, and you have to register and tell them how long you're planning to stay and what your intentions are, et cetera. Once in a while, someone gets lost in Ringer and is found, bedraggled, befogged, and dehydrated, resulting in a photo-and-interview op as the third or fourth story in the local Channel 8 six o'clock news broadcast. But that's only once in a while.

I registered, said I didn't plan to spend more than a couple of hours there (true), and they whizzed me through the gates into the big parking lot on the north side of the main trail. I had hidden the Finn 23 in the trunk, but I needn't have bothered. No one cared.

Only two other cars were inhabiting the Ringer parking lot. Having given myself three hours to get in and then back out of the Ringer Wilderness, I grabbed the Finn and put it into a belt holster that I'd bought at Rogelio's gun shop. I had my winter boots on, a good pair of thermal insulated gloves, a cap with earmuffs, and a parka: I had overdone the outerwear business, but that's what someone who sells insurance does without thinking. An insurance agent will overprepare for any eventuality. I also brought a flashlight—can't remember why—and a bottle of water and my cellphone in case of emergencies, but my thinking was that with the Finn, there wouldn't be any such emergencies unless I *wanted* them to happen.

The firmament was overcast, one of those Great Lakes depression-inducing skies, and a light semi-sleety snow was falling, making dull drooping sounds as it dribbled itself through the trees, mixed with the occasional cry of a flightless bird, a pheasant or a partridge seeking shelter. I followed the Maple Trail #2 into the northern sector of the park and tramped off the trail and headed east, away from any other day-trippers or winter campers who might have heard or seen me. I wasn't sure where I was headed, and I didn't know what I was looking for, but I felt that I would know my prey when I found it.

After about half an hour's walk through some thick under-growth, in the middle of a forested nowhere, I took out the Finn and looked for something to shoot. Taking aim, I fired a bullet at a spruce tree that was in my way. Some of the bark sheared off where I hit it, and the sound echoed for a few seconds after I fired. Two more birds raised an avian alarm, and, close by me, I heard the frightened chittering and churring of a critter, probably a humble chipmunk. I aimed at the sound and fired. I must have hit it, whatever it was, despite the chances of a direct hit being a million to one, because the chittering abruptly stopped, silence took over from the echoing gun blast, and the snow-covered forest floor a few paces ahead of me displayed a sudden blood spatter and tiny bits of internal organs and fur.

At that moment I came to my senses, and I thought: *What am I doing here? Who am I? What am I becoming?*

I was not myself. As quickly as I could, I walked out of there to my car, and in haste I drove home.

I'm not asking for sympathy. This is not that kind of story. I'm just telling you what happened.

21

A FEW NIGHTS LATER, AS I HAPPENED TO PASS BY LENA'S BEDROOM door, I heard her say, "Daddy, could I talk to you for a minute?" I knew Pete wasn't around—he hadn't had dinner with us, as he usually did—so I pushed against the door, entered her room, my daughter's inner sanctum, which I never visited these days without an invitation, and I sat down on her bed. She was in her desk chair with a biology textbook open, and her desk lamp streaming down incandescent light onto a translucent anatomy page illustrating the human body: the circulatory system, the lymphatic system, the intestines, the reproductive equipment (the body was that of a male)—all that. I felt an intense but microscopic shiver.

The bedroom of a high school girl—well, I can only speak about Lena's—has a fierce softness, a kind of animal seductiveness decorated with pictures of horses and cats, track team trophies (Pete's, and another one for her from middle school), earbuds, stuffed animals, iPhone, clothes on the floor, and an air of funky perfumed expectation. The room can seem to be both a refuge and a jail cell. With its lavender and pink and purple surfaces, the world is softened by these artifacts and made more feminine than it actually is. I had the impression that Lena's room was enfolding me, and I wondered whether Pete felt that way when he was making love to her in this room, in the bed I was sitting on, or when they were making plans for the future together. I don't know how else to say this: sometimes Lena felt more to me like a sister than a daughter, my sibling and not my child. Occasionally I felt I understood her as a brother understands a sister and not as a father understands his daughter. Then that feeling passed, and I was her father again.

She was wearing a Kingsboro High School T-shirt, faded blue jeans, and her brown hair was held back in a ponytail, and she was barefoot, with toenails painted green. She had been crying, and when she cried, she looked slightly like Cheryl, her mom. They scrunched up their eyes in similar ways. Her cheeks were red, and crumpled tissues littered her desk on either side of the biology textbook. A relic from her childhood, a little unicorn, gazed down at her from a bookshelf. My heart thumped in my chest out of sheer paternal pride and sympathy and desolation. She's a beautiful girl, my daughter, and I don't want anything bad ever to happen to her while she's under my care, but I know that no parent can protect anyone forever from the tornadoes, the gunshots, the head-on collisions, the hungers, the disappointments, the betrayals, the lies, the pandemics, the solitudes, the sexual assaults, the manias, the accusations—all the dark nights of the soul and the body. No soul, no dark nights. There she was.

"What's going on, kiddo?" I asked.

She grabbed a tissue and blew her nose, and I reached out to squeeze her other hand.

"Oh," she said. "It's nothing. It's everything." Everything is everything and nothing when you're her age.

"Such as?"

"Pete got the letter from Ohio Wesleyan last week. His application was rejected. His grades haven't been so good lately, and he's kinda blaming me. He says, and I quote, *love takes too much out of me.* Love saps his strength, he says. I mean, is he blaming me for the time we spend together? For the amount of time that we—"

I held up my hand. "Don't say it."

"Yeah, okay, I don't want to offend your parental sensibilities," she said, a practiced sentence. "But, you know, I mean you're aware we've been sexually active. We make love. We have been known to fuck, pardon my language. You know that."

"Uh-huh," I said, giving her a neutral smile. I don't like obscenities coming from anyone, including my daughter or, for that matter, me. "It's no secret. I always figured you loved each other, so it was sort of okay. You do, right? You do love each other?"

"Well, we did. I don't know about now."

"No?"

"Well, what can you say to a guy who tells you that you wear him out?"

"You ask him why he's saying that. You ask him who else he's seeing. You ask him if he's cheating on you. You ask him if he's lying to you."

"I did all that."

"What'd he say?" I asked. Sometimes you have to ask a question you don't want the answer to.

"He didn't answer. He just looked at me. Then, well, yeah, he admitted some things."

"Then that's your answer."

"I always thought we'd be together forever. I did, Daddy, I really did. You know: Childhood sweethearts? Love for forever? Doing things according to the rule book? There are marriages like that."

"Yes, I know there are."

"And I thought we'd have one like that. We'd be together, like, forever."

"So what are you going to do?" I asked.

"It's not what I'm going to do, it's what's already happened."

"Which is?"

"Well, I'm going to wait to see if he gets accepted to Ohio

State, or at least *somewhere,* and we'll go together there, if he makes good on the promise to give up the girl he's also been seeing. Which he admitted. Maybe it was nothing. He says that all she wanted was to fuck him, nothing else. I mean, he already said he's sorry, as soon as I found out. He has already promised. He'd been texting me and said it was all over between him and her, and it was only once or twice. He's coming over here tonight. We're going to talk and, you know, like that."

"What's the girl's name?"

"Louella. Everybody calls her Lulu. That's the name for a hooker. I'd like to kill her, but I don't know how I'd do it, and anyway I'd get caught."

"Right. Kiddo, I'm sorry to tell you this, but a lot of men are dogs. A lot of them cheat. They just do. It's in their—our—nature."

"You never did."

"No, but—"

"And Mom did, with Burt."

"Well, maybe she couldn't help it."

"I feel so bad for Mom. I mean, she's living with that guy because she wanted to be under his thumb, and she fell for him, because she liked to look at him, and he's just a creepazoid and a nothing, and now she has to clean him up and like that."

"Yes."

"I feel so sorry for her. Love got her into that mess. I wish you'd be nicer to them."

"Well, I try. It wasn't love, she says. I asked her. Anyway, I've done my best. So I've been shoveling money in their direction, as much as I can."

"Really? She didn't tell me."

"Really."

"Oh," Lena said. "There's another thing."

"What?"

"Pete. I mean, he's really sorry that he cheated on me. *Really* sorry. You wouldn't believe how sorry he's been."

"How sorry is that?"

"This sorry: In school today? In the hallway? By my locker? After all his texting yesterday, he got down on one knee this afternoon and asked me to marry him. Other kids were watching him. They couldn't believe it. I couldn't believe it. We're going to be the talk of Kingsboro High. I mean, he didn't have a ring or anything, but that was what he asked. 'Would you marry me?' I was blown away. I mean, you married Trey on the spur of the moment, didn't you?"

"Yes and no. So what did you say?"

"I said, 'Thank you.'"

For a moment I was speechless. I heard the clanking of barbells from the basement. "You thanked him?"

"Yup."

"What'd he say then?"

"He asked me if that was a 'yes.' I told him it wasn't. Then he asked me if it was a 'no,' and I said it wasn't that, either. I mean, he's pretty fucked up if he gets down on one knee in a high school hallway asking me to marry him. The boy is super-confused. He could've waited at least until the school day was over. He could've waited until we were in the parking lot or something. But he didn't. This is going to get us into the school newspaper. I mean, I guess I'm discovering how impulsive he is. I'm getting so I don't trust him."

"Right."

"And I'm feeling sorry for Mom, over there in that crappy house where the roof is leaking, with Burt. They put saucepans down on the floor to collect the water. It plinks."

"She'll manage."

"She might not. And I feel sorry for you, Daddy."

"For what?"

"You're in the middle of all this. I mean, I've got this problem with Pete, and Burt started calling Joe names because he's gay and now Joe wants to bulk up, and you've got to pay money to Burt and Mom, and the blood test says you're going to murder somebody. I just hope it isn't me that you murder."

"The blood test is a fraud. It was just a thing that happened. I'm not going to murder anybody."

She gazed down at the book, at the anatomy lesson. "I sure hope not," she said.

THE DINNER THAT NIGHT PROVED TO BE AWKWARD. FAMILY LIFE! I HAD put some music on the audio system, the Oscar Peterson Trio, softly in the background, but that didn't help. Bobby the rat was back again in our midst, perched quietly on Joe's shoulder. Bobby was the most compliant member of our household and the least trouble and quite easygoing, for a rat. They made quite a pair, Joe and Bobby. They had bonded. Joe was wearing a T-shirt with its sleeves cut off to show off his biceps, which were enlarging as per expectation, but I still felt confused about how his workouts and musculature were going to help him in being gay. Of course, he would need to be brave, but I didn't see the connection. It's easy to become confused in these matters where young people are concerned, when they're working at becoming one sort of person after being another sort of person.

Trey and I had prepared this chicken-and-pasta in pesto sauce, one of those dishes you basically can't mess up, but you couldn't deny that wholesale drama had presented itself at the dinner table, Pete having proposed marriage to Lena earlier in the day. He and Lena were seated at one side of the table, Trey and I on the other, and Joe and the rat were at the head of the table like the king and his consort, and I was watching Pete carefully. He and Lena weren't holding hands or anything of that nature, as they often had in the past. He was wearing a sweatshirt and jeans, and his face alternated between polite smiles and hangdog dejection resembling the expression of a losing politician on election night. I didn't blame him for feeling despondent, and I didn't blame myself for being quietly angry at him: he'd been caught cheating on his girlfriend, my daughter; he had proposed marriage and had been deferred; he was failing, or almost failing, some of his courses, and had been rejected from Ohio Wesleyan (would he even graduate from high school this coming spring? another puzzle); his absent-minded single-parent mom didn't seem that interested in him, which was why he spent so much time over here, with us; his prospects, in other words, were not bright. At that moment he reminded me of Dr. George B. Graham III, the loquacious vagrant who had accosted me in the Kingsboro town square to bend my ear about the British Royal Family. His posture conveyed the sense that the cards were stacked against him, events would turn out for the worse rather than the better, and nobody would ever offer a helping hand. He looked like that.

"More chicken in pesto?" Trey asked him, passing him the dish. Other people's troubles flowed calmly over her. If you were in Trey's company during the apocalypse, the apocalypse would simply not happen. It would go somewhere else.

"No, thank you," Pete said.

"I heard you proposed to Lena today," I said, trying to sound chipper.

"Yeah." He nodded, as he continued eating his salad. He was a handsome guy, I have to admit, even when he was disconsolate.

"You did?" Trey asked. "How exciting!" She turned to Lena. "You didn't tell me! What'd you say?"

"I said, 'Thank you.'"

"Oh. So you didn't agree to it? Well, you're both so young," Trey observed, trying to smile. "It's a big decision."

"He did it halfheartedly," Lena said, while Pete visibly squirmed. "He didn't quite mean it."

"Could we talk about something else?" Joe asked. It was around then that the Oscar Peterson Trio CD ended.

"Such as what?" his sister asked, turning in his direction.

"Well, I got us another movie at Famous Discount yesterday. They're selling them for two dollars apiece now. *Alien vs. Bimbo.* Anybody want to see it?"

Collectively, as one, we all answered him. "No," we said. Then Lena announced, "I don't like bimbos and I don't like movies about them. That's sexist."

"You're so *liberated*," Joe said scornfully. "So *excuse me* for my antifeminist microaggression. So what's your opinion about aliens?" Bobby the rat gazed at Lena with equanimity. "Are you opposed to them, too?"

"Aliens? They're okay." Lena smiled at her brother. "Depends on the alien, of course."

"Aliens are cool," Joe opined. The rat on his shoulder seemed to nod, a yes-rat. "And so are bimbos. Depends on the bimbo, of course. There are good and bad bimbos. You can't generalize. That's group-ist."

"Anyway, I've got to study," Pete said, wiping his mouth, and I assumed he meant that he would study here with Lena, my daughter, who had once been his prop and support. And that was the dinner. Trey and I started to clean up, and the kids went to their rooms.

A COUPLE OF HOURS LATER YOU COULD HEAR THEM UPSTAIRS MAKING love in Lena's bedroom. Lena and Pete's study session apparently

had concluded, and now this had started. No wonder he was getting failing grades. Given what had just transpired between them,
wouldn't she deny him this? Maybe she had been moved by his
marriage proposal. What was studying compared to being in love
and having adolescent sex whenever you wanted to have it? What
had happened to shame, to stealth, to the shy in-the-shadows lovemaking of previous generations, when youngsters hid away to
consummate their yearnings, huddling and fornicating in cars or
in forests or in the slatted shadows under the bleachers? Those
times were over, except for the Christian Nationalists and the evan-
gelicals and their ilk, all the Old Believers who were eager to
enforce the traditional repressions. They yearned for the iron fist
and gruesome punishments; they hoped for interminable waiting
for any pleasures at all. How they all loved abstinence! However,
for the New Believers in the mainstream, shame was passé. If
people wanted to have sex, they had sex right now, as long as it
was consensual, and they didn't care who knew about it.

Trey and I exchanged glances, and she shrugged. She was dry-
ing the last of the dishes, and when she finished, she returned to
the living room to read the novel her book club would discuss next
month. She put on some other music: Joni Mitchell, to drown out
what was going on upstairs. She had delicate sensibilities, Trey
did. Joe had retreated to his bedroom and was writing an English
paper, aided and assisted by Bobby the rat. His sister's sexual activities did not interest him or break his concentration. That left me,
alone, beside myself.

I climbed the stairs and slunk into my bedroom, where just
to the right of the closet door I had positioned a rocking chair,
a side table, and a reading lamp across the room from the bed. I
brought an insurance trade magazine up with me, but I had no
intention to read it. My daughter was quietly moaning, and I could
tell that she was making an effort to be discreet (couldn't they

have gone somewhere else? apparently not), but the effort didn't
seem to be working out, and the moans were interspersed with
little cries, which might have been genuine cries leading to tears.
I don't know. Please don't think ill of me for this, but I had come
to think that sex was overrated, all of it, and everything connected
to it, except love.

To add to all that, the headboard was banging against the
wall—that cliché of bad movies and books. When I listened to that
sound, it reminded me of Morse code. Maybe it was a message. I
don't really know Morse code except for SOS, but when I closed
my eyes I imagined I knew it and thought that maybe the message was about my mother, or, as I drifted into a semi-somnolent
state, was actually from my mother. What was she telling me?
My mother has been dead for several years—breast cancer and
alcoholism got her—and she worked as a grade school teacher
before the cancer hit, and though she got a nice going-away send-
off, everybody knew that she had Stage Four, and before very long,
it was curtains for my mom, who everyone said was a saint and
whom I loved despite everything. For me she wasn't a saint, just
my mother, and when she died, I grieved as a good son would, as
did my brother, Earl, who lives in Milwaukee, with his wife and
three kids, one of whom is on the spectrum.

Half-asleep, in headboard-banging Morse code I heard my
mother telling me that she was all right and had taken up water-
color painting in the afterlife. She told me that I should let things
happen as they will happen and not to worry. She said that Joe
would be okay and would have a good life and that Lena would go
to Ohio State but not marry Pete, and that was all right too, it was
just in the nature of fate, and she—my mom—praised my having
married Trey, that good woman who worried about the environ-
ment so much that she sometimes didn't flush the toilet after uri-
nating so as not to waste water from the rivers and aquifers. Mom

said that the afterlife was very much like life here on Earth except that slowly but surely she was dispersing into atoms and wave particles and knots of energy, and that someday, infinitely in the future, through countless aeons of supernovas and black holes, the particles of energy of which she was a mere and minor collection would recombine, and we would all be here again, living our lives over as Nietzsche had predicted we would, but better, with slight déjà vu inklings that we had been here before, so we would all be better and happier the next time around and not make the mistakes we had made previously.

When the banging of the headboard stopped and quiet descended, my mother departed. I seemed to recover from my drowsiness. Two hours later, I went to bed myself, kissed Trey and told her I loved her, and I wished her sweet dreams as I always do, and she wished the same for me, and she told me she loved me, and we drifted off to sleep, with our arms around each other, me in my pajamas and she in her nightgown.

THAT NIGHT I DREAMED THE STRANGEST DREAM: I FOUND MYSELF IN a city, bombed out and dead like the cities you see in the newspapers, the neighborhoods destroyed and desecrated by wars, and in this city where no one lived, I seemed to see the ambling dead, neither zombies nor horror-movie types, but naked people, for the most part, a few of them clothed. They walked in a wayward manner, but some of them appeared to be advancing in reverse: like a Michael Jackson moonwalk, going backward while stepping forward. The city had been emptied of all color and therefore of all desires, and when I tried to engage one of these people in conversation, the figure—I couldn't tell what this person's gender was—said, "You don't belong here." Nearby, dogs were making love in the missionary position.

No one likes to hear about another person's dreams. I have been warned by my instructor, Eleanor Sandler, and my fellow writers at the Blueberry Hill Writing Workshop not to include them here. But, reader, if you have made it this far in my tale, you will understand how frightened and secretly emboldened I was by this dream, and you will understand that when I opened my eyes and saw a figure standing in the doorway of my bedroom, naked, looming, unlit and therefore faceless, an alien intruder, someone from the stillborn dead city who might have an intent to do us harm, I felt my stomach clench in horror. Still in a fog, half sleep and half enraged fear, I reached over to the drawer of the bedside table, and, pulling out the trusty Finn, I aimed it at the threatening figure in the doorway. I am convinced that I was not fully awake. I tell myself that. Reader, you may remember that I have informed you twice that Peter Potter, my daughter's boyfriend, was a sleep-walker, but perhaps you have forgotten that small unimportant fact just as I did in the moments before I aimed the gun at the figure in the doorway and fired one bullet at him.

Part III

Let me explain what I do here. I don't want to confuse you any more than absolutely necessary.

—Eugene Ormandy

22

WHEN YOU GO THROUGH THE EMERGENCY ENTRANCE AT THE KINGS-boro Hospital and are standing under the fluorescent lights, you notice the low hum of complicated muffled machinery, and behind that hum, resembling the low note on a pipe organ, comes the clatter of metallic instruments dropping into little trays. From down the hallways you can hear groans and entreaties for help, but before all that, you have to get past the triage nurse, who decides who gets admitted and in what order and how fast. That night the woman behind the desk was, according to her name tag, Suzanne. She had brown hair falling to her shoulders, and she looked at us with a kindly skeptical expression. I was there with Trey, who had driven the car, and Pete and Lena, who sat in the backseat.

"Your name?" Suzanne, the triage nurse, asked me.

"Brock Hobson." I showed her my health insurance card.

"And why are you here, Mr. Hudson? What's the trouble?"

"Hobson. Chest pain."

"Aha! Chest pain." She typed something into her computer while gazing at the screen. "And did you bring your vaccination card?"

I SHOULD EXPLAIN THAT I HAD MISSED PETE BY ABOUT THREE FEET, though the bullet had gone clean through a blue lampshade and then had passed through the floral wallpaper to lodge in the drywall near the bedroom window. In the ensuing melee, I explained to a frightened and suddenly awake Trey what had happened, and I apologized to Pete for the two of us being asleep (well, he had been fully asleep while ambulatory, and I was in what they call a twilight condition) so that I had taken a shot at him, thinking he was a criminal intruder from one of those movies where the entire family is slaughtered by a murderous psychopath. My own shock was mixed with shame of the fear-and-trembling variety that I had nearly murdered someone. As I sat or stood there—can't remember exactly which—with the Finn still in my hand, I felt a painful tightening in my chest. Black wings descended over me. I couldn't breathe. I had the taste of copper in my mouth. Cold sweat began to emerge on my forehead. I was dizzy. I felt the world receding, but I did have one thought: *At least I fooled the algorithm.*

"I think I'm having a heart attack," I told Trey quietly.

"Why'd you shoot at me?" Pete asked me.

"My apologies. Please. I'm having a heart attack," I repeated. "It hurts."

"I think he was asleep," Trey said to Pete, who was still standing there in our bedroom, naked as a jaybird. "Here, honey," she said to me. "Get your clothes on. Should I call 911?"

"I don't know. I can't think."

"You shot at me," Pete insisted, peevishly. He wasn't going to let it drop. "With a gun."

"I woke up and saw you and thought you were a burglar or a racist—I mean *rapist*—or something," I said to Pete, the first of what would be many apologies. "I'm very sorry. Truly. Mistakes were made. I was still half-asleep and I thought you were someone else." I did my best to stand up and to put on the clothes I had worn yesterday evening and had tossed on the chair. My head was full of random thoughts while a chain tightened around my chest. "I think I might be dying."

"You could have killed me."

"But I didn't. Yes, I'm sorry. I *said* I'm sorry. Won't happen again. But what about me? It's me who's dying."

"Well, no harm done," Trey said, ever the optimist. "Too much talk about aliens! We've got to get you dressed now."

"Daddy, what's going on?" Suddenly Lena was in the room, half-clothed. So much nakedness in this household! Maybe too much. I didn't like all this nudity and shameless display, but even in my clouded condition, I realized that unclothed bodies took second place to my chest pain.

"I'm having a heart attack."

"I heard a loud noise, a bang," she said. "What was that?"

"He shot at me," Pete said, sounding a bit miffed. "And now he's having a heart attack. It's like a happening."

"Well, we better get him to the hospital," Lena said calmly. "We can do it faster than 911 can. I'll get the car out of the garage. I just gotta get dressed first."

That's when Joe appeared, wearing boxer shorts. It was true that the weight lifting and the Muscle Milk were starting to get results. For a high school sophomore, he was quite buffed. He rubbed his eyes. "What's all this?"

"Nothing," I said. "Go back to bed." I had put the Finn into the drawer of the bedside table. I would get rid of it if I survived the heart attack. What a night!

"Kind of coincidental, isn't it?" Trey said. "You shoot at Pete, but it's you who's down for the count."

"Don't say that," I said, but I needed help to walk, and so Pete took my left arm and Joe took my right arm, and they helped me down the stairs and into the front seat of the idling car.

In the ER they took a blood sample from me, hooked me up to a tube that sprayed oxygen into my nostrils, gave me an X-ray and an EKG, and the resident doctor on call, Dr. Peterson, listened to the fluttering of my heart through his stethoscope. He asked me detailed questions about how I was feeling—better, thanks—and then went away without commentary, leaving me in the ER's little examining room with Trey. Lena and Pete had waited for a while until a doctor or nurse or someone had told them that I wasn't going to die just yet and that it was okay for them to go home.

"The thing I don't understand," Trey said to me, as we waited there in the examining room, me stretched out in the sort-of bed, and Trey sitting in the nearby chair, "is how come you kept that Finn in the house."

"My mistake. I should have thrown it away, pronto. I admit that now."

"It was almost like you were trying to fulfill a prophecy. From Generomics."

"Naw. It wasn't that. I mean, people do keep handguns in their bedrooms, you know," I said, feeling bleary. "I couldn't figure out what to do with it, and I didn't want to shoot anybody, especially him. The gun happened to be there. Pete's a nice guy. He's almost family. It just happened."

"But it's not like you to do that."

"Well, what is?" I asked.

"What is what?"

"What is like me?"

"Good question. I don't really know," Trey said. "But not that. Cleaning out the garage—that's more like you."

Maybe this wasn't the right time or place to define my character. People could summarize me at my possibly upcoming funeral if they wanted to. They could start working on the eulogies at any time. Right now I just wanted to know what was going to happen to me medically, my death prospects and so on. How soon would I prove to be mortal? After another interval, minutes or hours, during which time I thought about cremation versus full burial and what flowers I wanted on the altar, Dr. Peterson reappeared, wearing the ghost of a smile. "Well," he said, standing to the side of my sort-of bed, where I was lying in wait. "It seems you're okay."

"I don't feel okay."

"Maybe so. But the blood test we gave you can indicate a heart attack, and it didn't, and the X-ray shows nothing irregular, and the EKG is normal, mostly, though you do have a left bundle branch block, which I'll explain, but the circulation seems to be fine otherwise."

"So what am I feeling?"

"You've been having an extended panic attack. There's too much adrenaline in your system. Your blood pressure is wacky. You're under some stress, I think, and your body switched on the fight-or-flight mechanism and apparently kept the switch in the on position. I'm going to give you some beta-blockers and a sedative to calm you down, but I think you should stay in the hospital overnight. Is there something that triggered this reaction?"

"He woke up and shot at somebody," Trey said. "Accidentally. Nobody hurt or anything."

"Oh my goodness," said Dr. Peterson.

"It was a mistake. How often do I have to say that? I was half-asleep," I said.

"No harm done?"

"Not this time," I said, "except to a lampshade. So I don't need to talk to a cardiologist?"

"Only if you want to pay a social call," Dr. Peterson told me. He was a wit. "The LBBB might have been a minor factor, but we'll give you another test, a molecular stress test, for that, tomorrow. Like I say, we'll keep you under observation tonight, and in a little while they'll wheel you to the room we've prepared."

"'As I say,'" I corrected him. You can't use a preposition in an introductory adverbial clause.

"What?"

"Never mind."

"Okay," Dr. Peterson said, putting his ballpoint pen back into his pocket. "I'm glad to tell you that the results were nonconcerning. I'll write this up for the doctors who will see you tomorrow. In the meantime, we'll get some people to wheel you to your room."

Trey waited for another half hour, and then we spoke of our love for each other, our gratitude that we were both still alive, and after that she called an Uber to take her home, as the orderlies or whatever they're called now came for me and wheeled me up to Room 346.

WHEN WE GOT THERE, AND ONCE I HAD BEEN HOOKED UP TO VARIOUS monitors, I noticed that Room 346 was not a single room after all (as I had been told that it would be). At rest in the other, fully occupied bed was a very large mound of humanity, who I saw at once was George B. Graham III, PhD, the learnèd vagrant who had accosted me in the Kingsboro town square some months ago and lectured me about the Windsors. Kingsboro: small world! You can't make this stuff up. Although we were still in the depths of night, he had his reading light on and was wearing his glasses as he perused *People* magazine. An abridged version of *The Decline and Fall of the Roman Empire* was on his tray table. He too was hooked up to various machines.

"Oh, no," I blurted out. "It's you."

"Dr. George B. Graham, at your service," he said, the words

rolling out of his mouth in little wet syllables. "Mr. Hobson, I presume?"

"Yup. What're you doing here?"

"Me? I'm dying."

"Sorry to hear it. What from?"

"I must be brief. Speaking tires me out. To answer your question, I am experiencing general systems failure. I have diabetes plus congestive heart disorder, acute pulmonary difficulties, along with a growing distaste for the farcical goings-on of our quote common humanity unquote. I am dragged down by the terrible imbecility of the crowd, the moronic masses, and oftentimes find myself without a shred of hope, personal or collective. I have lost my customary sparkle. Of course I am a solitary being. I have been a one-man show and all my life have played to a very sparse crowd. My heart appears to have given up and wishes only to close down the enterprise and fold up the tent and steal away. Fortunately, no one will miss me. My soul shall scuttle away into the cosmic dark, and only the minor gods will note my absence. It will be as if I had never been here. To return to the dust is a finality that I foresee with fierce joy. I am ripe for it. And ripeness is all, as the Bard would have it. Ah, yes: I seem to remember you from several weeks prior to this one, when we encountered each other in the dusk of an autumn day. You were your crepuscular self. Shadows were carved like deep age lines across your face at that hour. You gave the impression that you were thirty years older than you actually were, the sort of prematurely aged man whom only an early retirement would save from the ash heap. Indeed, now it comes back to me. I told you to ask your son what he wanted in life, as I recall. What did he say? What was his reply?"

"He said he wanted to be happy. I think he also mentioned wanting someone to love him and someone to love." I did not mention that he hoped for the demise of Burt Kindlov.

"Our hearts are God's little garden." Dr. Graham sighed. "Imagine! A boy, sixteen or seventeen . . . ?"

"Sixteen."

"Think of it. A boy at that age, his ship having embarked from its home port only a few years earlier, wanting to be happy! Wanting someone to love! Well, happiness, adolescents believe, may be *within their reach*. It's outrageous. But funny, too. Astonishing, their belief in happiness. Megalith emotions spur them on. Such a belief is one of the dreaded effects of late capitalism and hormones, as that exemplary scoundrel Prince Andrew has demonstrated."

"I'm not sure that my son believes in happiness."

"Oh, I can assure you that he does." Dr. Graham huffed and puffed for a moment. "They all do, the youngsters of today. Even those in the grip of depression."

"You sound tired."

"Little elf, I am more tired than you could possibly know. Speaking tires me out, though you wouldn't know that based on my verbosity. Any hour now I shall shuffle off into the welcoming gnomic darkness." His voice was increasingly raspy. "I myself am incubating a black hole. Adumbrating it."

"You look okay to me."

"Well, you know what they say about looks and their deceptiveness. Believe me, my systems are shutting down, including all the interior pumps and whistles. And yet I have no regrets. I am not embittered. Poverty has chastened me. You may tell them all that I've had a wonderful life."

"You're going to live for many more years."

"No, I'm not," Dr. Graham said. "And no one will miss me."

"I will," I said.

"Why?"

"You make me smile," I told him. "I enjoy your company."

"Thank you," he said and sighed. "And that reminds me of an

observation I have lately noted concerning an anomaly that has *worried* at me during these, my declining final hours. I have an idea that I will convey to you since you are here in person. I speak of the *exceptionally peculiar* names of elementary school teachers, such as 'Miss Hagburg,' or 'Miss Splettstaisser,' or 'Mrs. Heap,' or 'Miss Haarstick.' They were my teachers, these women with these outlandish, atypical, implausible names. And there's more: Mrs. Heap, who was a fright to all us third graders, both boys and girls, *referred to herself in the third person.* She also shouted at us, and her spittle landed on our desks. She even shouted about the weather. I never knew her first name. Perhaps she did not have one. Or perhaps 'Mrs.' was her first name. It's possible. Missus Heap, her given name. Growing up, I knew a scrawny and sickly child, 'Hercules Poindexter.' What a curse a name can be! Down there in the South they love screwball names. It's a form of rebellion. Such bizarre naming practices are the last gasp of the Confederacy. The strange and unsightly names of these women I have referred to reflect an oddity concerning the larger class of mostly unmarried pedagogues, nor do I exempt the unmarried men such as my shop teacher, Mr. MacDonald Heskett, who also had the oddest of names and who also, I might add, was from the South . . ."

But the sedative and the beta-blockers had taken hold of me, and I fell asleep as Dr. Graham lectured me on his theory of the odd names of elementary school teachers, his soft, rumbling voice coming to me almost like a lullaby or the faint and monotonous wash of ocean waves.

IN THE MORNING, A NURSE CAME IN TO TAKE MY TEMPERATURE AND my blood pressure, both of which were normal, and she informed me that I could go home after the stress test and appointed someone to pick me up. She gave me Dr. Peterson's prescription for beta-blockers. The hospital staff would take me to the hospital's front door in a wheelchair as per regulations, and from there I would proceed to the car. I called Trey on my cellphone; she said she would come to get me and could be there before long.

As I was getting dressed, I belatedly noticed that the other bed was empty, or "untenanted," as Dr. Graham would say.

When the nurse returned with a wheelchair, I asked her what had become of George B. Graham III, PhD.

"He's not here," she told me.

"Well, I can see that."

"I'm afraid that's all I can say."

"Did he die during the night?" I asked.

"I'm really sorry. No comment." She frowned at me.

"This isn't a press conference," I told her.

"We are not permitted to disclose the medical conditions of our other patients. That's private information for family members only. I'm sure you understand."

"He didn't have a family. You mean his death is a private matter?"

"If it was, it would be."

"If I had died, whom would you tell?"

"The *immediate* family. There are protocols in place. I'm sorry I can't tell you anything more about Mister Graham. Really sorry."

"It was Doctor Graham. He had two PhDs from Wayne State University."

"I didn't know that."

"He thought that elementary school teachers often have funny names."

The nurse thought for a moment. "He was correct about that," she said. "And here is your wheelchair."

. . .

AFTER THE STRESS TEST, TREY TOOK ME HOME. LIFE RETURNED TO normal for two months or so. I had calmed down and enrolled in a meditation class. I scanned the obits to find anything about Dr. George B. Graham III but could find nothing; occasionally I thought that he had been a ghost sent to instruct and comfort me. I grieved the poor man and offered prayers for his erudite, restless soul. Somehow I managed to catch up on my office paperwork. Pete forgave me for shooting at him, and by means of diligent study he was admitted to Ohio State University, as I had once been, and Lena declared that she would accompany him there— she was very careful about her word usage and did not exactly say that she herself would enroll at OSU with him. Sometimes when I returned from the office, I noticed that both Lena and Pete were wrapped in the strong stink of marijuana, but that is another story, as is their stoned repartee at the dinner table. Joe continued to bulk up; at times his muscular physique alarmed me. He didn't resemble himself anymore. He looked like someone in a magazine or on the internet. Was he taking steroids? I should have asked him. But events were continuing offstage, and I had not forgotten about Generomics on the evening when Cheryl, my ex-wife, called to tell me about a request from Burt. But I already knew about the request, from an email he had sent me.

23

From: kindlov48@gmail.com
To: Brockhobson3@aol.com
Re: A Dual

I have bene thinking about you. You bene on my mind sucker. How I despise you I can hardly stand it. People like you lower the quality of life hereabouts for everybody. Always have. Since first grade. Probably before you were born. I can't get rid of all the other lowlifes but with you I can do the honorable thing and challenge you to a dual. I know you got that Finn and I got a Glock so maybe it will be a fair fight plus I have a tremer and am currently in a wheelchair. If you refuse this I know you as the coward you really are. If you accept maybe I respect you. Maybe youre a card-carrying American after all but I doubt it. Cheryl dont know I am writing this so don't tell her. With you gone Kingsboro will be great again. You got any balls you will reply in the affirmative.

Sincerly, Burt Kindlov

Over the phone, Cheryl said to me, "He says he sent you an email, but he won't tell me what it says. I guess I could go to his computer and check it out."

"He's challenged me to a duel. I can send you the email he sent me. He sounds completely unhinged. He can't even spell 'duel' correctly."

"That's the brain injury." A pause followed. "On the other hand, he was never a good speller. Don't bother resending his email. I know what it says. He talks about you all the time. I can't get him to stop. He hates you. He blames you for everything. You're an obsession with him. Almost like love, except not."

"The leaking roof?" I felt my sciatica starting up, and a pressure in the chest.

"Yes. He blames you for that."

"His fall down the stairs?"

"Of course especially that."

"His tremor?"

"You name it, you're responsible. Honestly, Hobby, I don't know what to do anymore." Her voice did indeed sound rather desperate, and I felt a flare-up of the love I once had for her when she and I were in high school. The love had nowhere to go, so I tried my best to snuff it out but did not succeed. "Burt's got this obsessional loathing for you and says you're a disgrace. It's one of his favorite words. *Disgrace, disgrace.* It's right up there with 'fuck' in his word pantheon. You're really all he thinks about. I mean, he obviously can't go to work or earn money, so he sits around and curses you. All day! It's unbearable. He's especially bad during his physical rehab sessions. I mean, thank God we have some disability payments, but he repeats 'Fuck that guy' so often, it's like a mantra when he's trying to walk in the rehab facility using the parallel bars, each step, and the therapists ask him to please pipe down. His colorful language upsets the other patients. Maybe he's got a case of Tourette's? How should I know? Plus all the debts we're piling up. I'm sorry I'm going on like this. With the money problems and the disability, he hasn't been thinking clearly ever since his fall. Me neither. He wants revenge." She waited. "He wants it bad. Against you."

"Well, I'm sorry for you, but duels are against the law."

"Yes, I know. But I've had an idea. What if we humor him, you know, play along a little? Get rid of the obsession? He might calm down, become himself again. Go into self-rehab."

"That's batshit crazy."

"No, it only *seems* crazy."

"What is this, *High Noon*? You must be joking."

"Well, I am but only a little. The thing is, maybe we take him out in his wheelchair, somewhere way out of town, maybe at the wilderness park, and he gets to shoot at you, sort of, but with his tremor of course he'll be lucky if he can even pull the trigger, much less hit the broad side of a barn, and that's that, he'll have had his day, and we get on with our lives, and, as I say, that's *that*."

"And what about me? Don't I get to shoot at *him*? It's supposed to be a duel."

"You wouldn't do that, would you?"

"I wouldn't mind killing the guy. I wouldn't do it, but I wouldn't mind killing him."

"That's insensitive. Now you're the one who's joking. Those Generomics people really got to you."

"Hmmm."

"Well, I'm almost sure he'd stop talking nonsense if we go through with this. Maybe it would bring him to his senses. Rid him of his obsession, which is the point. Incidentally, are Lena and Pete smoking weed?"

"You noticed. Yes, they are. They suck on the spliffs in his Toyota and then come in here, reeking."

"Yes," she said. "I thought so. Over here, too. Shouldn't we do something? Maybe it's just a case of senioritis they both have. Or could you and Trey do something? I worry about drugs. And speaking of that, Burt has been . . . Maybe I shouldn't tell you."

"Go ahead."

"Have you heard about edibles?" she asked me.

"I have."

"He's gotten his hands on them, by mail order, and he says they help with the pain."

"I'll bet. I thought edibles made people calm and peaceful."

"Not with Burt, they don't. They just add to how deranged he is."

"Come to think of it," I said, "I think I'd *like* to have a duel with that guy. I'd enjoy it—guns blazing in the fresh air, out in the open, springtime. Bees buzzing around, blue sky, birds singing, flesh wounds, the blood spurt, halcyon days. Yeah, I think we should do it."

"Now *you're* kidding."

"Not a bit. You go tell him I said yes. We'll go on from there."

IN MY CALMER MOMENTS, I COULDN'T IMAGINE WHY BURT HATED ME. Sometimes in the mornings I would take walks in the town square, doing my best to identify the trees—oak, maple, linden—and the birds—sparrow, cardinal, chickadee—and I would think: *I'm not such a bad guy. I like to identify trees and birds.* I've paid my taxes, I've helped to raise the kids, doing the best I could with Lena and Joe. And Pete. I'm a God-fearing man. I've gone to the PTA meetings and have been attentive to the goings-on at our school board meetings. My business has helped people who have suffered losses from fires, windstorms, water damage, and collisions. I pay my office assistants living wages, complete with healthcare benefits, and on a regular basis I have given money to Cheryl and Burt. I give to charities. I teach Sunday school. Face it: I'm not a bad guy.

Nevertheless, Burt wanted me dead, and he wanted to do the job himself. Sometimes in life the urge to kill a fellow human being does arise. These things happen.

One late-spring evening, thinking that maybe the gunplay we were contemplating could after all be quelled by a heart-to-heart talk, I drove over to Burt and Cheryl's little house on the west side of town. It was a nice evening. Trees were leafing out, and I didn't have to turn on the car's heater. To get there, you have to drive past an auto junkyard, with the piles of rusting Chevettes, Pintos, Azteks, Cimarrons, and Pacers among others (I had provided insurance for many of these lemons), and then you pass by a strip mall where there's a daycare center, a rival insurance office, a dance studio, an Indian restaurant, a massage parlor, and a pizza parlor. After that, the real estate goes rapidly downhill. You see houses that look as if they've been abandoned even though they haven't been, houses with broken windows, yards with slop, trash, and pudder scattered everywhere, a landscape of poverty and neglect. When you see people, they gaze vacantly at you and your shiny undented passing car. Their expressions seem to say, "You're in the wrong place."

I arrived at Burt and Cheryl's house, 2164 Westfield Lane, Kingsboro, Ohio, a rickety little dump domicile set back from the road and projecting a subtle aspect of depression and squalor. You could almost smell the cancer coming from in there. I decided not to park in their driveway but to locate the car a block or so away and walk to the site of their former connubial bliss. Once there, I could see a light from one of their windows, and from inside the house came the sound of a radio tuned to an oldies station playing "Unchain My Heart." As an insurance guy, I can do quick estimates of a house and its possible failings: bad roof, drafty windows, dark brown shake siding missing in one or two spots and needing either a coat of paint or a staining, dead tree nearby, ready to fall smack on the house in a windstorm. With a place like this, vinyl siding would give better, more efficient protection against the elements and would be a better bargain. I could go on. Mold, for example.

I pressed the button for the malfunctioning doorbell—well, I was uninvited over there, after all—but as usual, silence greeted me. I went down the front steps and walked over to the north side, passing by a bathroom window, brightly lit. I stepped back. The light inside was so bright that if they turned their eyes to the window, they would see only reflections of themselves. They would not see me outside watching them, as my ex-wife ran a soapy washcloth over Burt's ruined body, sagging now from muscles that had gone from firm to limp. His entire body was wasting away. The lawn where I stood was unkempt. From inside came the sound of a barking dog, no doubt a mutt who had sensed my presence outside the house.

Burt bent his head, and Cheryl soaped and washed the back of his neck and then his face with a regal tenderness that she had never shown to me during our marriage. His face was demure, the look of a man accepting love-bathing from a woman. She washed his shoulders with delicate swipes of the washcloth and then dried him with careful applications of a towel. She did everything for him that he could not do on his own. From where I was standing, I did not see in detail how she would bathe his genitals, but I knew, as I walked away, back to my car, that she loved him now and had never loved me in the same way, despite the evidence of our two children and their existence on the planet. For her I had been the reproductive means to an end. She had never shown me such physical or emotional *caritas*, if I may use that word. I had received it from Trey, but not from her.

I wept, and I hated him. A wreck of man, unemployable, unintelligent, a bully and a braggart, a man who had offered nothing to the world and who had called my son a faggot, and who was loved fiercely by my ex-wife, despite her denials. It would be my pleasure to remove him from our shared existence here on Earth.

Hey, I'm just kidding!

24

BY THIS TIME MY SUNDAY SCHOOL CLASS HAD BECOME A GROUP OF FREE Thinkers and were in open rebellion against me—at least the boys were. They were trying to be polite but they didn't believe me anymore. I considered quitting. But they were just kids—was I going to give up so easily? On matters of faith? Which people live by? But it turns out that you can't always counter faith with reason. The girls were also getting impatient: with me, with the boys, and with Scripture. Nerves were on edge. And Easter had turned out to be a particularly knotty time of year: the questions were more pointed on the subject of Christ's resurrection. I was encountering skepticism about the life after death: what it was like, had I been there, would there be fast food and video games? For that matter, would there be *anything*?

I said we wouldn't need fast food in the afterlife because we would be pure spirit, and they asked me how I knew that. Had I been dead yet? If so, what was it like?

I had been explaining to them about the Gospel of Matthew, Chapter 28, where Jesus appears after he has died and been reborn, and Luke 24:36, where something similar is going on, and where Jesus appears as a spirit, and Billy Tarbox, who was often the first person to speak up, just put his head down, and, speaking not to me but to the table, said, "He didn't hang around? He didn't stay? After he was dead and then came back?"

"Who? Jesus?"

"Yeah, him. It says he was there for a little while, and then he left. How come he didn't stay? They were his disciples and stuff. Like his posse."

"Well, he didn't have to be there for long. All he had to do was prove that God is . . . Well, he had to show that life and love can defeat death."

Jake Goetz had stopped raising his hand. He would just speak up whenever he felt like it. "Mr. Hobson," he asked, "where's Heaven?"

"Well, the Bible says that Jesus ascended into Heaven. So it's up there, somewhere."

"Up where?"

"I don't know. Somewhere."

"You're supposed to know."

"I don't know everything," I said. "We have to accept some things on faith."

"So if you believe this," Tommy Edie said, "like we're supposed to, and someone came along and, like, shot you, would you go into Heaven?"

"I don't know," I said. "I hope so. But I don't plan on getting shot."

"Nobody plans on that," Sally Horns said. "But it happens sometimes anyway."

AFTER MUCH SEARCHING AND COVERT INVESTIGATIONS, I FELT I HAD found the right place for a duel between Burt and me: a meadow out there in Ringer Wilderness Park, which you could reach by means of a dirt road that almost invisibly attached itself to County Road 2a on the park's southern border. It had to be accessible by road, since the only way that Burt would get there was by automobile and wheelchair. On crutches, even with help, he couldn't make it down a single city block. This was a guy who couldn't put on his own socks. In every respect, the location was ideal: remote, flat, unencumbered by flowers or other unnecessary decorative distractions—and it was public property.

Now the only barrier was my family; I would have to persuade them of my good intentions in having a duel between Burt Kindlov and myself. I could foresee many of their negative arguments. They would say that Burt and I were behaving childishly, or like characters in a novel by someone from the olden days like Tolstoy (no, they probably wouldn't say that), and they would argue that dueling, as I have already noted, was illegal, and that someone could be hurt or, who knows, possibly wounded or killed. And then what? Crime and punishment! They might claim that dueling is not a practice that Christians should engage in, although they had done so in the distant and recent past. They would say I was being impulsive. Was that really true? Of course I could keep the whole thing a secret, but I don't like secrets and had decided to tell everybody everything.

So on the appointed evening, at the dinner table, following our main course of beef stew and salad, I said, "I have a little announcement."

But by this time, Joe, Lena, Pete, and Trey had brought out their iPhones from their pockets and were texting god-knows-who-or-what. I disapproved of iPhones at the table but had lost that battle many times. Bobby the rat was dozing on top of Joe's head, and Pete and Lena were sitting side by side but not holding hands, making me wonder if the romance was over, and Pete had brought some orientation materials from Ohio State to read, and Trey was deeply involved with Lena in some discussion of policy at Knoblauch County Park.

I said, "I'm going to have a duel with Burt Kindlov out at Ringer Park, only it won't be a duel, more like a pretend duel."

"You are?" Trey looked up at me. She was worried. "Why?"

"Because he wants to."

"Somebody could be hurt."

"I don't think so. He has a tremor and his eyesight isn't the greatest. I wouldn't worry."

"You wouldn't shoot him, would you?" she asked.

"No, probably not."

"Oh. Okay. Promise you won't shoot him?" I promised. She went back to the text she was sending. After a moment, she said, "That Finn has brought us nothing but bad trouble. There's good trouble and bad trouble, and this is bad. I wish you had never taken that blood test."

But someone *had* been listening: Joe. He searched my face, as they used to say. "Are you gonna kill him?"

"No. I just said I wouldn't."

"Why not?"

"I don't want to. I just want to scare him and put a stop to his crazy ranting."

"He doesn't scare."

"Well, he was the one who challenged me to a duel, and I don't want to look like a wuss."

"He's a space cadet, Dad." Joe started to smile. "This is so cool. The blood test said you'd kill somebody, and now Burt has challenged you to a duel, and you could get lawyers at Dawes, Walling to defend you, and like that. It'd be like *a free murder.*" He finished up what was on his plate while the rat watched him eat. "You should do it. Hey, can I join you? I want to go out there. I'll be your second. What did Mom say?"

"She said he's got a one-track mind on this subject and I should pretend to have a duel with him, but no one should get wounded or anything."

"So do it," Joe advised me. "A guy wants you to fight him, so you fight him. Can I go with you? I'll shoot him if you don't."

"No. That's not what Christ tells us to do," I said. I was touched by his efforts to enter the fray on my behalf.

"Christ didn't live in the twenty-first century," Joe told me. "And he never owned a handgun."

25

THE DAY OF OUR DUEL DAWNED CLEAR AND WARM, WITH A SLIGHT
overcast. Any day, rain or shine, was a good day to pretend-shoot
in the direction of Burt Kindlov, who had it coming and deserved
a good scare, after which he would reform himself. I called down
to the office to tell Amanda Edmonds and Sheila Holzer, my assistants, that I wouldn't be coming in (bad cold, whose effects I imi-
tated by sneezing and snuffling), and I dressed informally, donning
some old jeans and a plain black T-shirt, the way I imagined Death
himself would dress up. I brought along a sweatshirt in case it was
chilly. I carried the Finn to the car gently, as if it were a colicky
infant. Outside, it being late May, the birds were screeching and
warbling and in general making a commotion, enough to wake
you up and get you out of bed and into your dueling gear. No
point in dawdling: time and tide wait for no man when there's a
shoot-out scheduled at an appointed hour. It pays to be prompt.
This is one of my cardinal rules.

Insurance agents *cannot* be late for appointments. It's bad for
business. We are early birds.

I had no fears and wasn't scared or even apprehensive. The
panic attacks had subsided completely. The absence of jangled
nerves was a surprise to me. My sciatica had not returned, nor had
the diverticulitis. I happen to believe in guardian angels and felt

their presence near me that morning, which perhaps accounted for the dead calm I felt.

When I arrived at the spot I had selected—I had emailed Cheryl and Burt a detailed map, with directions and a legend and a drawn compass pointing north—I removed myself from my car, which I had parked just off to the left of the dirt road, in a cleared space where park rangers could stop if need be. The only vehicle I had seen upon entering twenty minutes before had been an official one that had apparently been vandalized by somebody, no doubt a fun-loving teenager who had removed the decal "R" from "Ranger" so that the Jeep's hood sported the words PARK ANGER. A good joke! But the park, out here, off the service road, had no trace of anger, just a deliberate morning calm.

Because spring had arrived, the air was filled with tree pollen, as I surmised. I began sneezing uncontrollably, not faking it this time, and the sound of my noisy vocal extrusions was soon mixed with the rattle of a bad muffler on Cheryl's rusting butterscotch-colored Datsun as it made its way toward me down the service road. My wheezing and the wheezing of their car silenced the nearby birds. No wildlife would come anywhere near us. When they finally pulled up next to my car (which I had washed and waxed, a contrast to their rust), Cheryl, the driver, turned off the ignition. The out-of-tune engine dieseled for ten seconds or so before it finally stopped, making the dying noise characteristic of automobiles whose owners had neglected their proper care. The car also gave off a bad smell of burnt oil on the engine block. I was amazed that the Datsun still could start and run. Some cars are naturally heroic and refuse to give up. They are like old dogs in love with their masters.

Cheryl, my ex-wife, got out on the driver's side, and she waved at me cheerfully. Apparently nothing serious was about to happen after all—just a couple of boys playing with their weapons. I watched as she came around to the passenger side and removed a wheelchair from the car's backseat. She unfolded it. The wheelchair had gray duct tape in a horizontal line across the seat. On the reverse side of the backrest, Burt had attached an American flag. I was not surprised. In our prior conversations he had often bragged about his patriotism. "I love this country more than you do," he had once informed me. "I have always doubted your patriotism. Me, I've got a hard-on for the Stars and Stripes."

After opening the passenger-side door, Cheryl helped Burt out of the car and into the wheelchair. He was wearing a white cowboy hat. I think it was a Stetson, but I can't claim to be an expert on such matters. Nor was I certain whether his headgear was of the ten-gallon variety. The hat gave him courage, I believe. I noted also that he was wearing dark glasses, cowboy boots, and a T-shirt with another flag of our nation on it. The flag made a bold statement on his behalf. Here was a true American.

As Cheryl helped him into the wheelchair, I noted that Burt was clutching his Glock 45. The Glock is a superior firearm—good competition to the Finn I now owned, thanks to Generomics. At the same time, I saw that Burt did not seem to be his usual feisty self. He appeared to have been napping.

"What's up with you?" I asked him. He did not deign to answer.

"He's high," Cheryl said to me. She winked. "Completely stoned. He got a little nervous this morning. Drugs help. And he's had a few beers."

"Isn't," Burt argued with his customary eloquence. His head snapped back, and he may have opened his eyes, but you couldn't tell with those dark glasses. "I ain't so twisted that I can't shoot at you."

"Are you interested in killing me?" I asked him.

This question threw him for a momentary loop. "No," he said, at last. "Hurt you, though."

"Why?"

He appeared to take a split-second nap before becoming lucid again, whereupon he said, "Can't stand you, all your ways, your ███████████████████████████████, your ████ son, weak assholes, the way you ████████████████████████ and . . ." His head slowly lowered. He mumbled, "Get rid of people like you."

"Maybe we should call it off," I suggested. "This doesn't seem fair. Burt's woozy. He sounds like a stroke victim. Talk about fish in a barrel! It wouldn't be aboveboard."

"Oh, he just needs to get it out of his system," Cheryl said. She was quite cheerfully upbeat. At that moment it occurred to me that we were engaged in a slightly insane enterprise that against the odds also made a kind of common sense. You couldn't explain it in reasonable terms. You just had to do it. It was like faith. Sometimes emotions get you out in the middle of nowhere and cause you to wave a gun around. I had been reading up on duels on the internet and had learned that every duel in history was the result of strong feelings on each side. Drive-by shootings have a similar logic, as does urban gang warfare. We were not alone in our respective manias, Burt and I. Besides, tradition was on our side. I had also learned that duels still occur here and there, but in secret, like cockfighting. Read up on Aaron Burr and Alexander Hamilton's 1804 duel if you doubt me, or go to the famous musical about them, and consider their contemporary descendants in Chicago and Detroit demanding payback.

Everybody these days is getting fiercer, and we were no exceptions.

Behind me, I heard another car pulling up. I did not at first recognize the make or model but could eventually see that it was an old dark blue Ford Fiesta. The car shut off, and the driver came out: my son, Joe, wearing a muscle shirt. He was strong and quick and soon was at my side.

"How'd you get here?" I asked. "What are you doing here? How'd you know where I was? You shouldn't be here. You should go back home. This is no place for you."

"Sure it is. I borrowed Donny's car," he said, looking serious. "Did you forget? You told us where this would be." I had forgotten that I had done that. "Trey and Lena and Pete weren't listening. But *I* was." Now he smiled. "Besides, I told you: if it's a duel, you need a second. You know: an assistant. Here I am."

"I wish you hadn't come," I said.

"Anyway, the point is, I got here. What's wrong with Burt?" Joe asked, gesturing at him. "Oh, hi, Mom," he said, waving at Cheryl.

"Hi, kiddo. What're you doing here? You shouldn't be here. Did your father ask you to be here? And by the way, Burt's high as a kite," Cheryl said. "And a little drunk. It makes him feel like a man again. He needs that, poor guy."

"Don't call me that," Burt slurred. "I ain't poor. I've got riches you can't see."

"You can't shoot at him if he's high," Joe told me, looking down with pride at his own adolescent bulging biceps. "It's against the code of honor."

"Where does it say that?" I asked.

"In the rule book," Joe told me. "Also he can't wear glasses. It's against dueling rules."

Cheryl bent down and took off Burt's glasses. Immediately he squinted, and I saw that his eyes were wildly bloodshot from his intake of intoxicants.

"Well, okay," Burt said. "We gotta measure off ten yards or fifty paces or whatever."

At that moment I was really beginning to wonder what would happen and if anybody would get killed. However, and not to

drain away the suspense of this story, you can tell that I didn't die
because I'm writing this now.

TO MAKE A LONG STORY SHORT, WE MEASURED OFF APPROXIMATELY
fifty paces, though paces are hard to measure if you're sitting in a
wheelchair. Eventually Burt was satisfied with the placement of
his chair—he nodded, and the cowboy hat on his head nodded
with him—and I found a place to stand just outside a cone of
shade cast by a spindly maple tree.

"Don't you think it's about time to call this off?" Joe asked me.

"I don't think so," I said. "Once you start something like this,
you gotta go through with it. I'd never hear the end of it if I quit
now. This is about honor. Okay, move out of the way."

Following my order, Joe took himself off to a space behind the
maple tree, where I couldn't see him.

"Who fires first?" I asked.

"Coin toss," Cheryl told me, taking a quarter out of her jeans
pocket. "Burt, you call it."

"Heads," he said, pronouncing the word so that it sounded like
something else. Cheryl tossed the coin up into the air and followed
its arc to the ground.

"Heads it is," she said. Probably I should have been standing
there to verify her call, but I trusted her. Why would my ex-wife
lie about a thing like that?

However, at this point it did belatedly occur to me that Cheryl
would have quite possibly liked me to be dead, or at least wounded
and in pain, and that this entire charade had been her idea and that
she had forced Burt to go along with it. But no: that wouldn't have
been like her, the mother of my two children. I was just imagining things.

"Burt," she said, "you fire first."

The man raised his Glock and squinted at me, but his hands shook, at first slowly and then more violently, maybe from excitement, plus he was stoned goofy and barely awake from the edible he had consumed, and, who knows, bathed in the universal love, so when the gun went off, the bullet went so far afield up into the blue sky and off to my left that only a passing errant bird would have been endangered if one had been there in the line of fire. The truth was that with his tremor, Burt couldn't aim at all. He would never hit me, no matter what. I was safe and felt peaceful, inside a plastic bulletproof shield, as it were. We were just boys at play, a couple of aging, sporting Americans enjoying ourselves, and Cheryl knew that.

"Go ahead. Try again," I said. Burt looked at me strangely. Cheryl said no, that was against the rules, but I had a point to make, and Burt seemed willing to go along with my suggestion. With even greater difficulty this time, he raised the Glock again, and when he fired, he hit a patch of ground fifty feet or so to my right, causing the dirt to jump up. The Glock made a terrible sound echoing among the trees, I must say.

"Want another chance?" I asked. "Try again? Third time's the charm."

"No," Cheryl said. "That's enough."

Burt looked over at her. "I need help."

"That's against the rules," I said.

"Hey, I'm disabled," Burt informed me, "thanks to you, asshole. Cheryl, honey, w-w-w-w-would you lend me a hand?" His speech was terribly slurred, as usual, and you could hardly make out what he was saying; I wondered how many beers he had been slurping down in addition to the other intoxicants he had already consumed. I don't mean to make fun of his speech defects, but he did sound like a half-human creature in a carnival sideshow. What a wreck he was! His bravery was all a sham. He was less brave than I was and was now on the slippery slope of substance abuse. Everybody's life is a shipwreck at certain times but right now his was the worst I'd seen for many months.

Cheryl got herself behind his wheelchair and grasped the Glock and, for all I know, might have aimed it at me and helped him pull the trigger (though I doubted that she really wanted to kill me— well, anyway not then, because of the money she needed), but at that moment another gun went off behind me: my son, Joe, firing in our direction, and hitting one of the spokes of the wheelchair with a loud *whing* before the bullet went off harmlessly into the ground. Cheryl dropped the Glock into Burt's lap and scampered off to hide herself.

"Oh, Jesus," I shouted. "Joe, stop it. Where'd you get *that* gun?"

My son came out from behind a tree. "It's Donny's," he said, holding the pistol in his right hand. "His dad gave it to him. Anyway, Mom was going to shoot you."

"No, she wasn't. I know her. My God, you could've killed her. Okay," I said. "That's enough fun for one day. Show's over. Everybody's going home. Now. Give me that gun."

Joe handed the gun—a revolver—over to me. "Wait," Burt said. "You got to shoot at me. Those're the rules." By now, Cheryl was sort of creeping back.

"Actually, no, I don't," I said.

"Go ahead," he slurred. "Do your worst. I don't care no more."

"I've already done it," I said.

"Go ahead, kill me. Blood test says you will."

"No," I said. "I'd rather not."

"Go ahead," he insisted. "You got the right. Shoot me. There ain't nothing left to kill."

No, I don't have the right, I said to him and to Generomics and their blood test; *no,* I said silently, to Dawes, Walling; *no,* I said to myself, calling forth my superpower, which was forgiveness and bringing the dead (me and Burt, and Cheryl, and Joe, and maybe Lena and Pete) back to life; *no* to the Finn and the Glock and the eye-for-an-eye honor code that had brought us out there, and *no* to everything and everybody who had spent so much time and energy telling me who I was and what I was going to do and what I should do based on the "data." No one was ever going to tell me what to do again. Call it my Ringer Wilderness resolution: it turned out that I was my own man, and exiting from the park, I threw the Finn into the forest, though maybe I should have dropped it into a marsh where no one except the geese could ever find it. Freedom was what I felt. Freedom from them all. Eventually I would give the gun Joe used back to him, and he would give it back to Donny, who would give it back to his father, who might (or might not) notice that it had been fired. Maybe he wouldn't care. Ours is a violent country where a single bullet rarely matters.

The point is, I am still alive and grateful to life.

Thank you, Jesus.

26

IN THE FALL PETE AND LENA WENT OFF TO OHIO STATE AND MOVED into a furnished student apartment in Columbus whose rent I paid for. But even with my help, they didn't have much money, so Pete found a part-time job in a lumberyard, where he met a pretty payroll accountant. They fell in love, and Lena left her classes mid-semester and moved back here to Kingsboro to recover from his infidelity. Pete dropped out of school. Meanwhile, Lena grieved. My poor, sweet daughter: from behind her bedroom door I could hear her crying but could rarely comfort her, although I tried, because in the long run I believed she would be better off with-out Pete. All the same, I cooked for her and helped her with her transfer application to Vermeer College, where she'll be starting next semester. (It's a better school than OSU.) As for Pete, I don't know what happened to him or where he is. I don't remember the name of the payroll accountant; that's how little I cared about her. As long as he loved my daughter, I liked him, and when he didn't love her, I didn't. They were riding a two-person love bicycle with training wheels, Lena and Pete, and then they separately dis-mounted. Pete went from being a member of this household to being a stranger concerning whose fate I am indifferent. But for a time he loved my daughter. His love gave her confidence, and she was stronger for it.

Joe may have a harder time of it, but he's now a remarkable

physical specimen, even with his silver hair. He pretends to be a Silver Surfer, but there's no surf here in Ohio and never has been. (The waves coming in from Lake Erie do not count.) Slowly and tentatively he is telling Trey and me about how he feels about being himself. He's taking a martial arts class and maybe someday will be a black belt. What's so strange is that he's a sensitive boy who now looks like a muscled-up high school warrior. Appearance, with him, is not reality. I can't quite put it together, because the way he looks is not who he is. This odd result is partly Burt's doing, all that taunting and name-calling. Well, I imagine that things will sort themselves out eventually.

Bobby the rat has been overeating and suffers from morbid obesity. There's talk of putting him on a diet. Fat as he is, he's not as alert as he used to be. The glazed expression on his rodent face is that of an unambitious and sated Thanksgiving guest.

Trey and I are happy together. We both got through the pandemic without getting sick, and she's back at work at the Knoblauch County Park. Business has picked up at my office. I have almost more to do than I can handle. Which is fortunate, because Cheryl and Burt still need financial help. I still give them money. Trey thinks I'm a fool, fortune's fool, she calls me, affectionately, but I can't let them fall into suffering, even if the suffering is of their own making and well deserved. Charity is maybe a bad habit with me, but it's who I am.

I simply don't know what to think about those two. She loves him, and I guess he loves her, in his brutish, disabled, stupid way. I just have to leave them to whatever lives they want to make for themselves, using the money I give to them and what they get from the government. Besides, she's the mother of my two children, and I know they love her.

I think this story has been about love and not about the blood test in the title. Oh, I almost forgot: last week I received a phone call from someone who sounded exactly like Al Pilensky. But this time he said his name was B. Lindstrom. I asked him what the "B" stood for, and he said it didn't stand for anything. When I asked him what he was calling about, he told me that he had the records right in front of him about my involvement with Generomics, and he thought I would be interested in what he had to offer.

"And what's that?" I asked.

"Well," he said before clearing his throat. "This is rather hush-hush. But we trust that you will be discreet. Our firm, Age on Reverse, is marketing a product that may interest you."

"Uh-huh."

"We are offering a substance, Hydroglaxcelinotar, that simply *reverses the aging process.* Unbelievable but true. Furthermore, we arrange matters so that people you once knew will return to your life in their original condition, this time as holograms hooked up to the mainframe. We are engineering matters so that the experiences that you once had as a youngster, *you will have again,* but this time you will know what you know now. You will not make the mistakes that you once made. You can live your life over again but without error, completely wised up. Think of it! This involves an accelerator machine similar to a supercollider, that can in effect take you back to a period when you—"

"Thank you," I said, before I hung up on him. I was in the living room. Trey was reading a magazine, Joe was downstairs playing *Call of Duty,* and in the background our audio system was tootling Tchaikovsky's *Romeo and Juliet* overture conducted by the great Eugene Ormandy. A soft light from the setting sun came in through the west window. And from outside came the sound of a cricket. Night was about to fall all over us.

Acknowledgments

My grateful thanks to Deborah Garrison, Steven Schwartz, Julie Schumacher, and Pua Johnson for their careful readings. I am grateful to Jack R. Vermilya, Jr., for telling me this story. Thanks to Dr. Jennifer Stern for medical details, to Dr. Robert Behrends for the Rezillify, and thanks, as always, as ever, to Liz Darhansoff. Thanks to Susan Brown.